Baby-sitters Beware

THE BABY-SITTERS CLUB

Baby-sitters Beware

Ann M. Martin

AN
APPLE
PAPERBACK

SCHOLASTIC INC.
New York Toronto London Auckland Sydney

The author gratefully acknowledges
Nola Thacker
for her help in
preparing this manuscript.

Cover art by Hodges Soileau

ISBN 0-590-22871-4

12 11 10 9 8 7 6 5 4 3 2 1   5 6 7 8 9/9 0/0

Printed in the U.S.A.   40

First Scholastic printing, December 1995

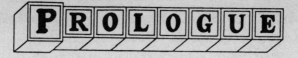

PROLOGUE

Shadow Lake

The name sounds full of mystery, and in fact there is a mystery attached to Shadow Lake. In the middle of the lake lies an island, where a wealthy family once built a huge house. The house burned down long ago, and the family just disappeared.

But I wasn't thinking about mysteries when I thought about Shadow Lake. If you've ever seen those bumper stickers that say THINK SNOW you know what was on my mind.

Let it snow, let it snow, let it snow! The moment I arrived at Shadow Lake, I was planning to engage in winter sports, big time. I wanted to ski, I wanted to ice-skate, I wanted to try out snowshoes, if I could get my hands (or my feet) on a pair. I was making Plans.

But my plans didn't include becoming involved in a major mystery. I mean, major — and majorly scary, too.

Now, the Baby-sitters Club, or BSC, of which I am president (more about that later) has been involved in its share of mysteries. But it wasn't until we were in the middle of *this* mystery that I realized we should be keeping a mystery notebook, too.

Too? Well, we already keep a club notebook. In it, we write about each and every baby-sitting job we have: who, where, when, what happened, and whatever else we think might be important. The club notebook is a handy reference tool. We're able to keep up with what is going on in the lives of our baby-sitting charges, and with any habits or changes we need to know about, such as allergies, teething problems, or phobias. We use the information to solve problems, too.

So it seems only logical that we should record our detective work. Reporting strange occurrences, and keeping a list of suspects and clues, could help solve the mystery.

Of course, as usual, when this mystery began, we didn't know it was a mystery right away. But once I realized what was happening, I decided to persuade everybody to think back and write up the incidents that marked the beginning of the mystery.

I can be very persuasive.

Kristy

We now have a BSC mystery notebook.

I just wish I'd thought of it sooner, because the BSC has, as I mentioned, been involved in a number of mysteries. Such as the time Dawn Schafer realized that there was a pet-napping ring here in Stoneybrook, when certain breeds of dogs started disappearing. Or the time we all had jobs at the mall as part of a school project, and we discovered that someone was involved in a lot more than shoplifting. And the time Claudia spotted a clue in a photograph and ended up helping to solve . . .

Well, anyway, you get the idea.

We know our way around a mystery. This mystery, however, was a lot scarier than the others. Creepy. Like something you see in horror movies.

It started as a simple vacation. But it ended up being a trip through our worst nightmares. . . .

CHAPTER 1

Kristy

Friday

The baby-sitter was in. I was at home with Andrew and Emily Michelle, who were in their bedrooms on their way to dreamland, and Karen and David Michael, who were in the den shrieking and giggling over a really, really bad horror movie on TV called It Came From the Snow. And I was thinking about snow myself. I was thinking what a horror it would be if it didn't snow in time for our trip to Shadow Lake.

The bony, gory hand shot out of the snow and grabbed the skier by the ankle. She screamed. She fell. She tried to escape, but it was no use. Slowly, slowly, the hand dragged her backward.

"*What* are you watching?" I asked, coming into the den.

David Michael and Karen both made a dive for the remote control. But I, a wily and experienced baby-sitter, as well as a seasoned older sister, had perfect instincts, impeccable timing, and lightning reflexes.

I reached the remote control first and clicked the mute button.

"It is an excellent, excellent movie," pleaded Karen, her blue eyes huge and maybe just a tad too sincere behind her glasses. "You can learn a lot about, about . . ." She frowned, thinking hard.

"About how not to go to sleep tonight?" I suggested. "About how to have nightmares when you do?"

"Oh, we won't have nightmares," said David Michael. "We've seen this about a million times."

"Gazillions," said Karen.

On the television screen, the skier escaped. She tried to run. The thing underneath the snow suddenly erupted out of it, right in front of her, holding one of her skis in each of its hands.

I jumped in spite of myself.

"Don't worry," said Karen reassuringly. "He doesn't eat her yet."

"And it's really fake-looking when he does," added David Michael.

I gave up. I handed the remote control back to Karen and David Michael and retreated with as much dignity as I could manage.

It was Friday night at the Thomas-Brewer mansion (my very large, blended family really does live in a mansion) and I, Kristy Thomas, thirteen-year-old eighth-grade student at Stoneybrook Middle School (in Stoneybrook, Connecticut), oldest daughter of the house, and president of the BSC (as I mentioned before), was baby-sitting for my seven-year-old brother David Michael, my seven-year-old stepsister Karen, my four-year-old stepbrother Andrew, and my two-year-old adopted sister Emily Michelle.

Emily Michelle was *not* watching the movie. She was asleep. I had just finished overseeing Andrew's bath, and he was enjoying staying up "really late." (I'd told him he could stay up as late as he liked as long as he stayed in bed. I'd left him sitting bolt upright, looking at picture books. I knew from past experience that half an hour later, he'd be fast asleep.)

My maternal grandmother Nannie was with her bowling league; Charlie, my oldest brother (who's seventeen), was at a basketball tournament; and my brother Sam (fifteen) was out on a date breaking up with his current girlfriend (although I didn't know that at the time). My mother and Watson, my stepfather, had gone to a Christmas party.

Shannon, David Michael's Bernese mountain dog puppy, was asleep on the sofa in the den. Boo-Boo, the cranky cat, was lurking somewhere in the house, no doubt waiting to claw whomever was unwary enough to walk by. The other assorted Brewer-Thomas pets, such as the goldfish, were, I hoped, in their proper places. And the ghost of Ben Brewer (an ancestor of Watson's), who — Karen firmly believes — lives on the third floor, was, I also hoped, in his room for the night.

That is my family. I've always had a larger than average family, but not always this large. I haven't always lived in a mansion, either.

When David Michael was just a baby, my father walked out on us. He turned up in California, and that was more or less the last we heard of him (I don't count random Christmas and birthday cards and gifts, usually late). We had a pretty tough time, Mom most of all, I think, but she held us together and things gradually improved.

Then, not too long ago, Mom met Watson Brewer. It was like at first sight, and love at second sight, and they ended up getting married. Watson was (and is) a real, live millionaire, so we Thomases moved from our tiny house on Bradford Court, where I'd lived my whole life, to Watson's mansion. Good thing it is a mansion, too, because Karen and Andrew, Watson's kids from his first marriage, spend every other month with us. Plus Mom and Watson adopted Emily Michelle, who was an orphan from Vietnam. Then Nannie came to stay with us, to exercise her organizational abilities and to help keep everything running smoothly. It usually does, but even when it doesn't, it's always interesting.

So that's my family.

Now. I have to tell you a secret. We live in a big house, and we all have our own rooms, and I love my family — but I was beginning to get cabin fever. We hadn't been away in ages. I was ready for a change.

I checked on Andrew, gently removed the books from his bed, pulled up the covers, and turned out the light. In her room, Emily Michelle was sacked out, clutching her Gund bear by the nose.

I wandered around the house restlessly. I wished that something interesting would happen. Anything. (Well, maybe not anything, I thought, remembering the monster movie that David Michael and Karen were watching.)

I decided to concentrate on the future. The near future. Just think, I told myself. In two weeks, you'll be at Shadow Lake.

Maybe that was why I had cabin fever — because I knew we were going away soon for a long weekend at the cabin, and I was in a fever to be there.

Although we'd just finished with Thanksgiving, and the Christmas holidays were around the corner, Watson had decided he needed to check on the cabin. I was thrilled. I loved Shadow Lake in the winter. I knew it was near downhill ski slopes, and I knew I could do some serious cross-country skiing, too.

Plus I was taking friends along.

The cabin at Shadow Lake is basic, but it is big. There are two bunk rooms that can sleep a dozen people each. The first time I'd gone to Shadow Lake I'd invited all my friends in the BSC, and everybody had accepted. We'd been able to fit everybody in, no problem.

Of course, I couldn't always invite all my friends to come along on our trips to Shadow Lake. But I'd realized recently that every time our family went away, big as it is, I'd been feeling sort of left out. I mean, Charlie and Sam have each other for company, and all the younger kids can play together. That left me alone in the middle.

So I was super pleased when Mom and Watson agreed to let me invite a few friends along for our winter excursion to the cabin. I'd already been talking about the trip at the BSC meetings, and at our next meeting, after I'd asked whether there was any official business (none), then asked if anybody wanted to come along.

Mallory Pike immediately shuddered and said, "No, thanks!"

Jessica Ramsey, who is her best friend, gave a shout of laughter. "Mal, there aren't any insects around in the winter. Not even at Shadow Lake!" We all cracked up.

Mallory gave us a sheepish grin. On her one and only visit to the lake, she'd been plagued by hordes of insects in spite of the fact that she had applied gallons of bug spray and was clothed from head to toe. She admitted, "I guess not. But anyway, I can't come because

11

I have to sit for my brothers and sisters both days that weekend. Mom and Dad are adding more insulation to the house. It's one of those do-it-yourself projects." She sighed and then added, "At least I don't have to help with *that*."

Jessi said, "She's telling the truth, because I am the second baby-sitter." (There are seven kids in the Pike family, not including Mal, so the Pikes always hire two baby-sitters.)

Shannon Kilbourne couldn't make it either. Shannon is an associate member, which means she takes baby-sitting jobs only when we're swamped. She doesn't usually come to meetings, but she happened to have a free afternoon that day. Generally, her life is planned *weeks* (or maybe years) in advance, around her extracurricular activities at Stoneybrook Day School, the private school she attends. *"Merci,"* she said with a shrug. "But the French club is helping out with the library sale at our school that Saturday."

Shaking her head regretfully, Mary Anne Spier said, "My social studies paper is due the Monday afterward."

Abby Stevenson, who lives one house over from me, grinned and said, "Well, count me in."

"Don't you have to ask your mom or something?'' asked Mary Anne, whose father is kind of picky about things like that.

Abby lifted her eyebrows in surprise. ''Sure, I'll ask her,'' she said. ''But it'll be okay. We can ski up there, right?''

I nodded and Stacey McGill said, ''Well, if my mom agrees to it, count me in, too.''

''Decent,'' said Claudia Kishi. ''Count me in three.''

So the four of us were going to Shadow Lake.

I could hardly wait. I'd already made my packing lists. Waxed my skis. Done a little research on the snowshoe business. Taken my ice skates in to have them sharpened.

Can you tell I was ready?

Only two things worried me. The first was Watson. He's had a heart attack. As heart attacks go, it wasn't a serious one, but any heart attack is bad . . . and scary. He'd recovered and he was following doctors' orders, such as sticking to new diet and exercising regularly. And he seemed to be his old self again, doing everything he'd done before the attack.

In fact, it seemed to me that physically, he was doing more and more. Was Watson pushing himself too hard? Would going to Shadow Lake be too much for him?

I told myself that Watson knew what he was

doing. That the doctors and my mother were keeping an eagle eye on him. But still, I couldn't help worrying.

The other thing, which wasn't that big a deal, was Sam. He and Stacey had once been very interested in one another. In fact, their romance had started on our first visit to Shadow Lake. Things had cooled off since then. Stacey and Robert Brewster are dating each other now, and Sam is dating someone else, too.

But I knew that Sam and his girlfriend had been having problems. And I also knew that Sam still liked Stacey, although I wasn't sure if it was in that boyfriend-girlfriend way. He did ask about her regularly, though, and it seemed to me that the more trouble he'd had with his girlfriend, the more he asked how Stacey was doing.

Sam has never been subtle.

What if the trip to the lake, where Sam and Stacey had first gotten together, rekindled their interest in each other? Or what if it did for Sam? Or just Stacey? What if someone got hurt? I mean, it was possible that the cabin could turn out to be Heartbreak Hotel, if you know what I mean.

I definitely didn't want that to happen. And I didn't much want to be around if it did. . . .

Oh, relax, I told myself now, returning to the den.

David Michael had put his hands over his eyes and was peering at the screen through his fingers. Karen had made her hands into "binoculars" and was watching the movie that way. They were both giggling.

"Kristy, hurry! You're going to miss the best part! The house catches on fire, and then it's buried by an avalanche, with her and the monster inside!" Karen shrieked.

What else could I do? I sat down to watch the movie.

The house on the screen started to burn.

"And I thought I had worries," I said softly to Shannon, patting her puppy head.

Shannon wagged her tail and licked my hand reassuringly.

CHAPTER 2

Jessi

Monday

It didn't take very long for me to figure out that Mal was not happy about having to baby-sit on the weekend that Kristy had invited everybody to go to Shadow Lake. In fact, she was complaining about it even before the Monday meeting of the BSC.

"Do you know what our basement is filled with? Insulation," said Mal bitterly. "Boxes of it! *Bales* of it! Tons of insulation."

"I can see you're warming up to the subject," said Abby, and slapped her leg in exaggerated glee.

Mal did not smile. She just gave Abby a long-suffering look and said, with icy dignity, "Ha, ha."

It was a Monday afternoon meeting of the BSC. Kristy was sitting in the director's chair, as usual, with her visor on and her attention divided between Claudia's clock and the watch on her own left wrist. Claudia, as usual, was on the prowl for junk food, which she keeps stashed in hiding places around her room. Abby was stretched out full length on Claudia's bed, with her feet dangling over the end and her arms folded, staring up at the ceiling. Stacey was pulling out the BSC treasury envelope, preparing to demand that we hand over our dues, since Monday is dues day for the BSC. I was sitting next to Mal on the floor, leaning against the bed and trying to look sympathetic.

Amazingly enough, it seemed as if Mary Anne was going to be . . .

Late?

Jessi

Nope. The door flew open and Mary Anne rushed breathlessly into the room.

The clock rolled over to 5:30.

Kristy announced, "This meeting of the BSC will come to order."

"Tigger," said Mary Anne breathlessly, referring to her tiger-striped gray kitten. "I could hear him mewing but I couldn't find him anywhere! Finally I figured out that he was locked in the hall closet."

"Did you get him out?" asked Claudia.

Mary Anne nodded. "I gave him a treat to show him it had all been an accident in the first place."

"Treats are good," said Claudia, holding up a bag of assorted Halloween candy.

"Dues are even better," said Stacey.

We groaned, but we all paid up. Dues might not be better than treats, but they are important (and they do sometimes pay for treats, such as an occasional pizza party for the club).

But I guess I should start at the beginning.

You may already know a little about the Baby-sitters Club, but in case you don't, we are seven experienced baby-sitters (plus two associates) whom parents can reach with just one phone call to Claudia's number, Monday, Wednesday, and Friday afternoons between 5:30 and 6:00.

A simple idea but a brilliant one, thought of by our president, Kristy. The club started out with four members: Kristy, Mary Anne, Claudia, and Stacey. Kristy and Mary Anne lived next door to each other on Bradford Court and Claudia lived across the street. Stacey had just moved to Stoneybrook from New York City.

In no time at all the BSC had more work than it could handle. That's when Mary Anne asked her new friend (who later became her stepsister) Dawn Schafer to join. Mallory, who was (and is) younger, soon followed as a junior officer, and so did I. I mean, I'm a junior officer too, and Mal's best friend.

Then after much back and forth about whether she would be happier staying in Stoneybrook with her mother and new blended family (which by then included Mary Anne and Mr. Spier), or returning to California to her father and brother and her father's new wife, Dawn at last decided to move back to California. Aside from missing Dawn as a friend, we soon discovered we were in the middle of a baby-sitting crunch. That's when Abby Stevenson, who had just moved into Kristy's neighborhood, was invited to join, along with her twin sister Anna. Anna said no, Abby said yes.

Jessi

We have two associate members. Shannon (Kristy's neighbor) and Logan Bruno, who don't often come to meetings, take sitting jobs when the rest of us can't fit them into our schedules.

Kristy is 1) Very Organized, and 2) Full of Great Ideas. As a result, the BSC is very organized, and has some unique things going for it. We meet regularly, and hand over dues every Monday. The dues are used for gas money for Kristy's brother Charlie (he drives her and Abby to meetings). Also, as I mentioned, the money's used for BSC pizza parties every now and then. We also spend the dues on our Kid-Kits, another Kristy idea. Kid-Kits are boxes that we've decorated (mine has an office theme) and filled with old puzzles, toys, games, and books, plus new stickers and markers and whatever else we think kids might like to play with. Even though most of the stuff in the Kid-Kits is secondhand, to the kids at our jobs it's all brand-new. And have you ever met kids who don't like playing with other kids' toys more than their own?

We don't take the Kid-Kits to every job. We save them for rainy days, or for kids who are in bed with colds, or for times when we think we might need something extra to help a job go smoothly. And you know what? They work, almost every time.

Mary Anne maintains the club record book, where she records each job and keeps a calendar of other things the BSC members do, such as my special ballet lessons in Stamford at Mme. Noelle's, every Tuesday and Friday afternoon after school. The record book also has a list of all our clients, with their addresses and phone numbers, plus any special information we might need.

Kristy runs a tight ship. Someday, I'm sure, she'll be running a bigger ship, such as a major corporation (or maybe Congress) in much the same way.

Of course, our success isn't all due to organization. We can also congratulate ourselves on being very, very good at what we do. (I'm not bragging, just stating a fact. We wouldn't be successful if we weren't good, would we?) I think one of the reasons the BSC is such a solid club is because we are all so different. I know you've heard it before, that opposites attract. But in this case, it's really true. We all get along, most of the time, even though our group is filled with pairs of opposites.

For example, Kristy and Mary Anne are best friends. It's true that they have a lot in com-

Jessi

mon: They are both short, each lost a parent early on, they are both very organized and responsible, and they both live in blended families now.

But Kristy is outspoken and outgoing and sometimes almost too blunt. She gets her point across, and she won't take "no" for an answer. (Although she certainly doesn't hesitate to use it as an answer herself!) Kristy, who has brown hair and brown eyes, wears a sort of uniform of her own — jeans and sneakers and a sweater or T-shirt. She is also athletic, and coaches a softball team called Kristy's Krushers, made up of little kids whose ages range from two and a half to eight.

Mary Anne is shy and not athletic. (I can't imagine her as a coach, standing on the field blowing her whistle and running a practice!) She is very sensitive and cries easily. Even commercials can make her cry. Unlike Kristy, who has always lived in a larger than average family, Mary Anne was the only child of an only parent for a long time. Her mother died when Mary Anne was just a baby, so Mr. Spier raised Mary Anne alone. He wanted to make sure that he did it right (and he clearly did) so he was very, very strict. It took Mary Anne awhile to make him see that she wouldn't be a little girl who needed little-girl rules forever.

Gradually he loosened up (especially after Mary Anne showed him how responsible she was already) and now she doesn't have to wear little kid clothes (or braids!) anymore. He's even calm about the fact that Logan (yes, one of the associate members of the BSC) is Mary Anne's steady boyfriend. In fact, her father is pretty all around reasonable these days.

And that's not just because of Mary Anne. Dawn Schafer had something to do with it, too.

How?

Well, Dawn and Mary Anne became best friends not long after Dawn moved to Stoneybrook, with her mother and brother, from California. Dawn's mother had grown up in Stoneybrook and was returning after she and Dawn's father divorced. Soon Dawn and Mary Anne discovered that Dawn's mom and Mary Anne's dad had been high-school sweethearts. They put their heads together and gave the old romance a new push, and it worked! Sharon Schafer became Sharon Schafer Spier, and Mary Anne and her father (and her kitten Tigger) moved into the old farmhouse where Dawn and her mom were living. (Dawn's brother Jeff had moved back to California before the wedding.)

Jessi

Since Dawn and Mary Anne were best friends, they were pleased that they could be sisters, too. Here's another case of very different people getting along. Dawn, who is tall and has long, straight blonde hair and blue eyes, and two holes pierced in each earlobe, is quiet but not at all shy. And she has very strong feelings about things. She's practically a vegetarian. She avoids all sweets (she calls sugar poison!), and is careful about what she eats. She's very environmentally conscious, too.

We miss Dawn, and I know Mary Anne misses her most of all.

Claudia and Stacey are best friends, too. They are both a little more fashion conscious than the rest of us. Stacey's sense of style has a New York spin to it, while Claudia's is more artistic. For example, for this early December meeting when most of us were in jeans and sweaters, Stacey (who is tall and on the thin side, with blonde hair and pale blue eyes) wore black leggings with cowboy boots, an oversized turtleneck sweater, and this cool black suede vest with pearl buttons. Claudia (who is Japanese-American with creamy, perfect skin, brown eyes, and long, straight black hair) was wearing leggings, too — purple ones — with black Doc Martens, red slouch socks, black bicycle shorts over the leggings, a big T-shirt with the words "This Might Be Art" scrawled on it in purple (I knew she'd made it herself), and an old black suit jacket of her father's, with the sleeves rolled up. Stacey had gone for your basic gold earrings. Claudia's earrings were purple feathers (she made those herself, too).

They both looked fantastic. I think they would have drawn admiring looks from people even on a crowded street in New York.

But even though they are best friends, like Mary Anne and Kristy, and Mary Anne and Dawn, Claudia and Stacey are very, very different.

For example, when it comes to school, Claudia would rather be anywhere else — maybe even the dentist's. She is not a good student, and she is what you might call a creative speller. Although she's an extremely talented artist, maybe even a genius, her teachers and her parents still insist, to her complete puzzlement, that other school stuff is important, too.

Claudia tries, but she often needs help. And her parents still go over her homework with her every night.

To make it tougher, Claudia's sister Janine is a real, live, academic-type genius. Even though she's only in high school, she's already taking courses at the local college.

But Claudia manages not to let it bother her, most of the time. She goes on seeing the world her way, making art, and appreciating junk food and Nancy Drew mysteries (two more things about their younger daughter that mystify Claud's parents). She's even managed to combine her love of junk food with her art, by organizing an art show based on junk food.

Claudia is the vice-president of the BSC, mostly because she's the only one of us who has her own phone line in her room. That lets us receive calls from clients and call them back without tying up anybody's family telephone line. Claudia doesn't have any official duties, but she makes it her unofficial duty to see that we are well supplied with junk food, plus a little healthy food on the side, for every meeting, something we all appreciate.

The health food is mostly for Stacey. It used to be for Dawn, too, and of course we all can eat it. But unlike the rest of us, Stacey can't eat junk, not the sugary kind, anyway. And she has to watch what she eats very, very carefully.

That's because Stacey has diabetes, which means her body can't regulate the sugar in her blood. She could get very, very sick if she isn't careful — even go into a coma. It also means that she has to give herself insulin injections every single day.

For a long time, Stacey's parents were just as overprotective of Stacey in their way as Mary Anne's father was of her. But Stacey finally managed to convince them that she could be trusted to take care of herself. And she does.

As BSC treasurer, she also takes care of our dues. Stacey is a math whiz, and good at other subjects in school, too. She's a little more sophisticated than the rest of us, most of the time. In fact, right now she's dating a guy named Robert who hangs out with a crowd at SMS that thinks they are too cool to talk to mere mortals. Robert's not like that, but Stacey was drawn into that crowd for a while, which caused some trouble in the BSC. Boy, am I glad *that* is all over!

Anyway, Stacey's an only child, like Mary Anne, but unlike Mary Anne or Kristy or Dawn, she's not part of a blended family. Her mother and father got divorced not too long ago. Now her father lives in New York City, while Stacey lives here in Stoneybrook with her mom. Stacey visits her father in New York often, so she maintains her New York cool. But then, it's hard to shake Stacey up. She's one of the calmest, most level-headed people I know.

Mal and I are the third set of best friends in the BSC. We are both in sixth grade and we both love horses and horse stories, especially the ones by Marguerite Henry. We also like mysteries, and we are the oldest kids in our families, which is a big help for a baby-sitter, experience-wise. But while Mal is the oldest of eight kids (including a set of triplets) I have just one younger sister, Becca, who is eight, and one younger brother, John Philip, also known as Squirt (he's a toddler). My aunt Cecelia lives with us, to help keep an eye on us since my mom went back to her old job.

Mal has blue eyes, curly reddish brown hair, and pale skin that burns and freckles easily. She wears braces and glasses and dreams of the day her braces come off and her parents allow her to have contact lenses. Mal likes to write and draw, and wants to be a children's book author and illustrator someday. She's already won prizes for her writing, and she even had a temporary job helping out a famous children's book writer who lives in Stoneybrook.

I like to dance. In fact, I want to be a ballerina someday. I get up every morning at 5:29 A.M., one minute before my alarm goes off, to practice my ballet moves at the *barre* that my parents set up for me in the basement of our house. I am a little taller than Mal, and thinner, and I have brown skin and brown eyes. I guess I'm inclined to wear ballet style clothes (Mal is a jeans and sweater person, more like Kristy). I often wear my hair pulled back in a bun, and leotards and leg warmers are fashion accessories for me as well as dance necessities.

Both Mal and I wear earrings because we were recently allowed to have our ears pierced, the first victory in our ongoing battle to convince our parents to treat us more like adults.

Meanwhile, we are the youngest members of the BSC and the junior officers. We're junior officers because we can't baby-sit at night, except for our own families. So we do a lot of afternoon and weekend daytime sitting, which frees the other club members to take jobs at night.

The newest member of the BSC is Abby Stevenson, who has a twin sister, Anna. They look alike — they are both medium height with dark curly hair and brown eyes and pointed faces — but Anna wears her hair short while Abby wears hers long. They both have contacts and glasses, and wear either one, depending on how they feel. Abby is our alternate officer, which means she fills in for other officers in the club when they can't make it to a meeting.

The Stevensons just moved here from Long Island, because Mrs. Stevenson landed a great new job in New York City, to which she commutes every single day — plus most Saturdays, and some Sundays. That leaves Abby and Anna pretty free to do what they want.

Come to think of it, I can't imagine anyone preventing Abby from doing exactly as she pleases. She's been in the BSC for just a little while, but she is what Stacey calls One Tough Cookie. She stands up to Kristy, and is as firm in her opinions as Kristy is. Abby loves jokes, especially puns. Sometimes she even makes them in two languages, because Abby speaks a little Yiddish. Yiddish is a language that was spoken mostly by Jewish people in Eastern Europe, where Abby's mother's family is from.

Abby's also a born athlete. I don't think there's a sport she doesn't play, and she seems to take to them all naturally. Right now she's playing on the soccer team. And she runs miles when she's not practicing soccer (or some other sport) to keep her competitive edge. I haven't seen Abby play soccer yet, but if she runs as fast as she talks, she should have no problem. She is always in high gear and high spirits. One other thing about Abby is that she has allergies to all kinds of things, including milk and many animals that have fur. (Her motto is: "Life makes me sneeze.") She also has asthma. Like Stacey, Abby has to be careful about what she eats, and she has to carry an inhaler with her at all times. An inhaler is a small, tube-shaped device. When Abby has trouble breathing, she holds it to her mouth and takes a breath out of it. It helps when she's having an allergic reaction, or feels an asthma attack coming on.

Shannon and Logan are our associate members. Like Abby, Shannon is a neighbor of Kristy's. In fact, she's the one who gave Kristy's family their Bernese mountain dog puppy, after the Thomases' wonderful old collie Louie died. The puppy was one of a litter that Shannon's dog had had. David Michael named the puppy Shannon, in Shannon's (the person's) honor.

Logan is not only a member of the BSC but, as you know, Mary Anne's boyfriend. He's definitely cute (Mary Anne thinks he looks like Cam Geary, her favorite star), plus he has a nice, soft Southern accent, and he's very easygoing. He's also a super jock. His main sports are baseball and track. It's good to know that we can count on Logan and Shannon in a pinch.

Like now. Kristy had just hung up the phone. "Mrs. Rodowsky," she reported.

We all grinned. The Rodowsky family is one of our favorites, maybe in part because the three Rodowsky boys for whom we baby-sit make it clear that we are their favorites, too. They've even gotten together with the Arnold twins and Matt and Haley Braddock and treated the BSC to lunch to show their appreciation. Shea, who is nine, is a terrific athlete and all-around good sport. Jackie, his seven-year-old brother, is so accident-prone that we call him "the Walking Disaster." (If he hits a home run, it's sure to break a window!) It never seems to bother him, though. He just grins and keeps going. And while we're not sure where on the athletic spectrum four-year-old Archibald Rodowsky fits yet, he, like his brothers, has red hair and a boundless supply of good humor.

Unfortunately, none of us could take the job. We all had other jobs or activities scheduled. So Mary Anne called Logan (naturally she knows his phone number by heart) and Logan took the job. Since he lives a few streets over from Reilly Lane, where the Rodowskys live, it worked out perfectly.

Meanwhile, I watched Kristy zip over to the window and back again three or four times.

"Santa's not expected until late December," said Abby, grinning.

Kristy rolled her eyes. "I can't wait that long. I want snow *now*."

"You still have two weeks," I said. "Anything could happen. Even a blizzard."

"Speaking of blizzards," said Kristy, "you should have seen this awful old movie David Michael and Karen were watching on TV Friday night. It was called *It Came From the Snow*. This thing kept lunging up out of the snow and grabbing skiers with its claws. It makes my top ten Worst Movies of All Time list. It was *terrible*."

"They loved it, right?" asked Stacey.

"Right," said Kristy. She glanced toward the window again.

"Snow is a kind of insulation," said Claudia unexpectedly. This is not the sort of fun fact that Claudia usually comes out with. She went on, while we all stared at her, "It helps keep the freezing weather from killing the plants. Janine was talking about it at dinner last night."

"Tell it to my parents," said Mal, almost crossly.

Jessi

"Do I sense a dislike of insulation here?" I teased Mal.

Mal said, "I told my parents about the trip to Shadow Lake. I told them that this time, there wouldn't be any insects. I told them I'd get to ski. And what did they say? *Insulation.* That's all they talk about."

"Well, at least you'll have me there," I pointed out.

Mal sighed.

"Thanks a lot!" I said, pretending to be indignant.

Mal sighed again. "It's not that, Jessi. It's just that the more I thought about it, the more I wanted to try Shadow Lake when it was bug-free."

"Well, don't worry," said Kristy. "We'll be going back. You can come with us next time."

A third sigh escaped from Mal, but at least she looked more cheerful. She managed to give us a small smile. "Okay," she said. Then she added, "Except that, with my luck, something really weird will happen on this trip, and you'll never go back."

Kristy held up her hands like claws. She made a hideous face. *"It came from the snow. . . ."* she intoned, and we all cracked up.

34

CHAPTER 3

Abby

Wednesday

Later, I realized that we were wearing nametags. Mine said, "HI, MY NAME IS ABBY STEVENSON. GET OUT OF MY WAY." I had written the last part on it after the meeting of the sports committee at SMS was over and Kristy and I were putting on our jackets to leave.

Abby

The sports committee is sort of bogus, but I figured I should be there, and I figured Kristy should, too. It wasn't too hard to talk her into going to a meeting to express her opinion. In this instance, it was a meeting to solicit student input about fund-raising for various sports programs at the school, and where the funds we were going to raise should be spent. I wanted to be there to put in a word for soccer. And Kristy, who'd been on the softball team, had a few words to say, too.

The teachers and coaches wrote down our comments and smiled and nodded and thanked us for our "input." I knew what that meant. They'd do what they wanted and we'd let them, unless we felt like putting up a big fuss about some really heinous use of the funds, such as painting the locker rooms plaid.

I'd stuck my nametag on my jacket. Kristy, who was wearing her collie cap, had put the nametag on the front of the cap. We were headed for the BSC meeting at Claudia's, goofing around as we went. At first, the sound of breaking glass didn't even register.

Then we stopped talking.

"Did you hear that?" asked Kristy.

"Yup," I said. "And as an experienced baby-sitter, I think it is definitely the sound of glass breaking."

"We're near the Rodowskys," said Kristy. "They live next door. Oh, lord, I bet Jackie's hit another baseball through someone's window."

She took off in the direction of the sound. Since I am unwilling at any time to let anyone leave me in the dust, especially Kristy, I took two giant leaps after her and caught up. We jogged around the side of the house and looked toward the Rodowskys'.

No one was outside. The backyard was empty. No red-headed Babe Ruths or Hank Aarons in the making. Not even the Rodowskys' dog Bo.

We turned like a precision marching team and sure enough, one of the side windows in the Rodowskys' neighbors' house was blasted to bits. But no baseball had done that damage. It had been something large. Person-sized, even.

Kristy and I exchanged a look and started walking back around the house without a word. No alarm was going off, but if someone had launched themselves (or anything large) through that window, we both knew without discussion that it would be better to call the cops and let them handle it.

Abby

We'd just reached the front of the house when I noticed an ancient, battered Ford Escort, that might once have been white, chugging up the street.

"Hey," I began, but before I could finish the thought several things happened very quickly — so quickly we didn't have time to freak out. (We had to save that for later.)

The front door of the house behind us banged open.

We both jumped about fifty feet into the air, although to our credit neither of us shrieked or screamed.

Then a man came barreling out of the door. I yanked Kristy out of the way (okay, so maybe we both yanked each other out of the way) and he hurtled past us across the grass, toward the car. He was a little shrimp of a guy, wearing a ski mask and gray sweats bunched at the ankles above scuffed jogging shoes. A gym bag was tucked under one arm like a football. And he was moving like a quarterback for the end zone.

But as fast as he was moving, his eyes seemed to take us both in, head to toe. They moved back and forth in the little circles cut in the ski mask, and it gave me the creeps. I felt as if I'd been photographed. Then he blinked and was gone, diving into the car. I heard him say something to whomever was driving. The car gave a lurch and the tires squealed.

"The license plate," exclaimed Kristy.

We reached the curb in time to see the license as the car sped out of sight, but it was covered with mud. Either those guys had been parking in a mondo mud puddle, or they fixed it that way.

Personally, I think they fixed it that way.

We turned again and raced to the Rodowskys' house. Kristy hammered on the front door while I rang the bell.

Mrs. Rodowsky opened the door. She looked very surprised. "Kristy! And . . . Abby, isn't it? You aren't baby-sitting today, are you? Because none of the boys are here — "

"No!" Quickly, breathlessly, Kristy told Mrs. Rodowsky what we had seen. Mrs. Rodowsky called the police, and they said they'd be there right away.

Then Kristy asked, "May I use your phone now, Mrs. Rodowsky?"

"Of course," said Mrs. Rodowsky. She excused herself to watch for the police. Meanwhile, Kristy dialed and said, "Hello, Claud? Kristy. Abby and I are going to be a little late for the meeting today. Start without us."

Trust Kristy to remember every detail.

Abby

The police were as good as their word. They showed up about three minutes later.

Why did it not surprise me that Kristy even knew one of the officers, Sergeant Johnson? She'd met him when Claudia had helped to solve a bank robbery, working from a clue she found in a photograph she'd taken.

Funny, but Sergeant Johnson didn't look all that surprised to see Kristy, either. He said hello as if Kristy were someone he talked to every day, then introduced his partner, Sergeant Tang. While she checked out the scene of the crime, he listened, his eyes intent, as we described what had happened.

When we'd finished talking, Mrs. Rodowsky confirmed that she hadn't heard anything until we'd showed up, acting like maniacs, on her doorstep. "Mr. Seger," she told Sergeant Johnson. "That's our neighbor's name. I barely know him, though. I don't even know his first name. He's not there that much and he's not very, well, outgoing."

"Have you noticed anyone around here lately who isn't one of your neighbors? Anyone who loitered in a suspicious manner? Has anyone come to your door and said they were selling something, or taking a survey, then asked you questions about your neighbors and their habits?"

"N-no," said Mrs. Rodowsky, frowning as she thought it over.

"Why?" I asked.

"Could be someone checking things out — casing the neighborhood — in order to plan a burglary," explained Sergeant Johnson.

"Wow," I breathed. "Excellent."

Kristy drove her elbow into my arm and said, "*Have* there been any other burglaries in the neighborhood?"

"Not to my knowledge," said Sergeant Johnson. (I guess it's a rule that police officers have to talk that way, as if they can't just say yes or no.)

At last the officers finished checking things out. Sergeant Johnson gave us his phone number so we could call him if we remembered anything we might have forgotten to tell him.

"Can we call you and find out what's happening?" asked Kristy.

"Sure," Sergeant Johnson replied.

"Are we going to see a lineup?" I asked. "Identify the burglar?"

"Maybe it won't come to that," said the sergeant. He nodded at Mrs. Rodowsky, and said good-bye. He and his partner got into their patrol car and drove away.

Mrs. Rodowsky looked at her watch. "Oops," she said. "I have to go pick up Shea and Jackie at the community center."

Kristy looked at her watch and exclaimed, "Are we late, or what! 'Bye, Mrs. Rodowsky!"

"Good-bye, girls," Mrs. Rodowsky called after us. "Be careful!"

"We will," I called back. To Kristy I said, "But I don't think we're going to witness two burglaries in one day, do you?"

Kristy said, "One is enough for me, thank you. Did you see how that guy looked at us as he ran by? It gave me the creeps."

"Definitely evil," I said.

Looking at her watch again, Kristy began to jog. I fell into step.

"Listen, we have a great excuse for being late," I said. "If you want, I'll write you a note. Or maybe we should've asked the sergeant for one."

Kristy didn't laugh at that. I should have known better than to make jokes about being late to a BSC meeting.

We jogged in silence the rest of the way. Kristy reached Claudia's front door ahead of me.

But I let her win. I figured it would make her feel better.

CHAPTER 4

Stacey

Wednesday

When Kristy and Abby came tearing into the BSC meeting that Wednesday afternoon, I thought the big news was that it had started to snow. It took a few minutes for the story they were telling to sink in. I mean, how many people do you know who have actually witnessed a real, live burglary? Not even in New York...

Kristy and Abby weren't all that late to the meeting. In fact, Kristy caught me goofing off, sitting in Claud's director's chair, tilting it back, pretending to give orders.

I thumped the front legs of the chair down so hard that they almost gave way beneath me. I jumped up guiltily. Amazingly, Kristy didn't even seem to notice. She only said, "Thanks, Stace," and dropped into the chair as if she'd just finished running a marathon.

"Well? What's the story?" Claudia demanded.

Kristy said, "We've been talking to an old acquaintance — Sergeant Johnson."

"Charlie got a ticket?" Mary Anne asked, wrinkling her forehead.

"No!" said Kristy. "Charlie's a good driver."

Abby burst out laughing. "I'll give you a clue — it would be a *crime* not to tell you what happened."

Claudia caught on first. "Crime! You're involved in a crime!"

"No way!" shrieked Mal. "That's great!"

Abby looked surprised and I almost started to laugh. Fortunately, Jessi demanded, "What happened?" That was all the encouragement Kristy and Abby needed to launch into their tale of terror. Well, maybe not terror, but it was pretty exciting and a little scary, especially the part about how the guy running out of the house had fixed them with his evil, ski-mask-framed eyes as he ran by.

In between phone calls, we talked the burglary over from every angle. But we couldn't come up with any clues. And both Kristy and Abby finally had to concede that they couldn't even be sure that they'd recognize the burglar without his mask.

"So what now?" asked Mal.

"Nothing," said Kristy. She suddenly looked serious and worried. Then she added slowly, "In fact, I don't think I'm going to tell anyone at home about this. I mean, I don't want to worry Watson or anything. I want him to take it easy and not overdo things, so he can enjoy the trip to Shadow Lake."

Mal suddenly looked glum. "I'm glad somebody's going to be having a good time that weekend," she said.

"I just hope it snows," said Abby. "I love to ski."

"Are you good?" asked Claudia.

"The best," said Abby. "We used to go up to Lake Placid every winter and ski our brains out. It's an Olympic ski center, you know."

"I know," said Claudia, looking a little put out. "I've been there." She added, "On the intermediate trails."

"Really? Not bad. I actually think that the trails there are a little tougher than anywhere else in this part of the country." Abby grinned. "I always try to do a couple of intermediates to warm up, before I head for the high country."

"How nice," said Claudia.

I stared at her in surprise. She sounded annoyed. Claudia has always been the primo skier in the BSC. Was it possible that she was jealous of Abby? Or did she think Abby was bragging? (I had to admit, it sounded as if she was, but then Abby is so incredibly self-confident that maybe she *wasn't* bragging.)

Mary Anne gave Claud a puzzled glance, too, but no one else seemed to notice.

I forgot about it the next moment, though, because Kristy said casually (very, very casually), "By the way, Stacey, I almost forgot. Sam said to tell you hello."

"Hello back to Sam," I said automatically.

The phone rang, and Kristy picked it up. "Hello, Baby-sitters Club," she said.

I was grateful for the interruption. While everyone else sorted out the details of the job, I let my thoughts wander back to a certain summer vacation at Shadow Lake.

Sam, Kristy's brother, who is two years older than I am, had been acting as if he were about six during the whole trip. He'd been teasing me, following me around, and calling me "dahling" in this stupid, exaggerated way. He was driving me crazy, but unlike a six-year-old baby-sitting charge, he couldn't be distracted with games, or sent off to take a nap.

I put up with it for a long time. Then Charlie had a little talk with his younger brother, and Sam worked up the nerve to have a little talk with me. We ended up dancing together at a dance at the Shadow Lake Lodge. And that led to dating, for awhile.

But it hadn't worked out. Not in any bad way or anything; it had just faded.

I was going out with Robert now. I liked — really, *really* liked — Robert. But for a minute, I couldn't help but wonder what would happen at Shadow Lake with Sam, wonder how he would feel and how I would feel. After all, that's where our romance had begun. And Kristy *had* mentioned that Sam had just broken up with his girlfriend. . . .

Abby began to make kissing sounds, and I jumped guiltily and felt myself blushing.

Fortunately, I blushed only a little before I

realized that everyone else was grinning at Mary Anne.

Mary Anne was a brilliant, beet red. "Stop that!" she said to Abby.

Abby wrapped her arms around herself. "Oooh," she said.

Jessi said, "Homework, huh? Study at the library, huh? I guess Logan's end-of-season football banquet just slipped your mind?"

"Okay, okay," said Mary Anne. "It's true. I want to go to Shadow Lake, but Logan and I also have a special date planned for Sunday night, to celebrate the end of football season."

"Gee, I'm shocked," said Kristy.

"I can tell," said Mary Anne, giving Kristy a wide-eyed, innocent look. Then she pointed at the clock.

We all looked at the clock. Then we looked at Kristy.

"Omigosh!" Kristy jumped up out of her director's chair. *"This meeting of the BSC is adjourned!"* she said.

She hurtled out of the room.

"Wait for me!" said Abby. "You're supposed to give me a ri — "

The door closed behind her.

It was six-ten.

Kristy had not only arrived at the meeting late, but she'd forgotten to end it on time.

Maybe that should have been a clue, of sorts, that the days ahead were going to be out of the ordinary, to put it mildly.

CHAPTER 5

Mary Anne

Thursday

No one ever believes it when something strange is happening to them. I don't. I think, I'm imagining this. I think, It's all just a coincidence. I think, Things like this don't really happen. Not to real people. But they do.

"Love letters?" asked Kristy in her best I'm-not-really-being-nosy voice.

I looked down at the folded white square of paper I'd found tucked in my locker. We were between classes at SMS and I hadn't seen Logan all day.

So while I didn't think it was really a love letter from Logan, I hoped it was a note from him, just to say hello. He does things like that sometimes. His thoughtfulness is one of the (many) reasons I like him so much.

I recognized Logan's handwriting the moment I unfolded the note. But the note itself didn't make sense.

"Mary Anne? Everything okay?"

Silently, I handed the note to Kristy. She read it, frowned and handed it back. "What does it mean?"

I looked down at the two words neatly written in the middle of the piece of white notebook paper, in what looked like Logan's handwriting: STOP CRYING.

"Stop crying about what?" asked Kristy. "Logan's not calling you a crybaby, is he?"

"No! Besides, I don't know what he's talking about. I mean, I don't remember crying about anything lately." (I didn't mention the old movie on television that weekend. I'd wept

51

buckets over the sad ending, but then, nobody had been around, so it didn't count.)

"Are you sure it's from Logan?" asked Kristy.

I studied the note. It looked like Logan's handwriting, but it didn't sound like Logan at all.

"N-no. No, I don't think it could be from Logan . . . could it?"

Kristy shrugged. "Maybe someone is trying to pull a psych."

The warning bell rang, and I hastily tucked the note into my backpack. Kristy said, "See ya," and disappeared down the hall. I slammed my locker shut and headed in the opposite direction, puzzled and a little disturbed by the weird note.

"Mary Anne?"

"Kristy? Is that you?" It was almost 9:00 at night. I was halfway through my homework. I pressed the phone more tightly to my ear. Kristy's voice was practically a whisper. "What is it? What's wrong?"

"There's someone outside our house," said Kristy.

"Call the police! Call Watson!"

"I have. I mean, I called the police," said Kristy and I realized that although she was whispering, she was very, very calm. The Universal Baby-sitter Emergency Response had taken over. "I'm whispering because I don't want whoever it is to hear me. I'm in the den. In the dark."

"Kristy!"

"Listen, I just want to talk to you until the police show up . . ." She paused. Then she whispered, "I heard someone around the side of the house."

In the background, I could hear a noise. I recognized it as the sound of a dog barking.

"Oh, no," said Kristy. "It's Shannon barking. She's just a puppy! What if she — "

Then her voice rose. "Oh no! Someone just broke the front window and Shannon's going in there. I have to go get her!"

"Kristy, wait!" I screamed. "Kristy! *Kristy!*"

But the line went dead.

I hung up and dialed 911 with shaking fingers. "Quick!" I screamed. "Someone is breaking in!"

"Where are you?" the voice on the other end asked urgently.

"Not at my house. At my friend Kristy Thomas's. I was talking on the phone to her. She lives at twelve-ten McLelland Road!"

There was a pause, then some static and voices talking in the background, and then the first voice said, "We just took a call for that address. Officers are on the scene now."

"Is she all right? Is she . . ."

Is she what? I thought. Dead?

I swallowed hard. "Thank you," I said.

I hung up. Then I dialed Kristy's number again. My palms were wet with sweat as the phone rang and rang. I was about to slam it down, run to Sharon, who was downstairs, and demand that she drive me to Kristy's right away, when suddenly someone picked up.

"Hello! Hello, Kristy?"

"Mary Anne?" Kristy sounded stunned.

"Are you okay? *What happened?*"

I heard Kristy take a deep, shuddering breath. "The police just arrived. Shannon's okay. I'm okay." She paused, then went on. "Someone threw a rock through our living room window."

"Oh, no!" I gasped.

"That's not all," said Kristy. "They spray-painted the front door. It says, 'YOU'RE NEXT.'"

"Oh, my lord." I didn't know what to say.

Still sounding stunned and oddly detached, Kristy said, "I have to go now. If I don't call you back tonight, I'll talk to you tomorrow. But don't worry. Everything is fine."

She didn't convince me. She didn't sound convinced herself.

I hung up the phone slowly, and realized that my hands were cold and shaky.

Needless to say, I didn't get much more homework done that night. I kept imagining Kristy, crouched in the dark in her den, whispering on the telephone while some lunatic lurked outside.

It was too awful to think about. But I couldn't put the picture out of my mind. I wanted to call Dawn, but I remembered that she was going out to dinner with her dad and stepmother and Jeff that night. They'd probably already left.

Logan? The words of the note crept into my mind: STOP CRYING. Logan hadn't sent the note. I was sure he hadn't.

But if he had, and if I called him, would he think I was a crybaby to get so upset over what had happened to Kristy?

Of course not, I scolded myself. Anybody would be upset.

But I didn't call Logan, either.

At last I gave up and decided to go to bed. I shoved my books to one side, wandered to the window, and looked out.

I peered at the sky, wondering if it was ever

going to snow. But the sky was clear, and I even saw a bit of the moon. We live in an old farmhouse on the edge of town. Our road doesn't have streetlights, so the moon seems to shine more brightly out here, without all the competition.

I leaned my forehead against the window — and froze.

Someone was standing in the shadow of the tree nearest my window.

I blinked, unable to believe my eyes. The figure didn't go away. It stayed there, motionless. The stillness, the watchfulness of it was very, very scary.

I don't know how long I stood there like that. Suddenly, I realized with a cold chill that I was outlined against the window by the light from my bedside lamp behind me. Whoever it was could see me clearly, could see my room, even though I couldn't tell anything about him.

I jerked back with a muffled shriek. I yanked the curtains together and stood there, breathing hard, as if I had been running. After awhile, I realized that I was clutching the curtains so tightly that my fingers were beginning to tingle. I let go of the curtains. I turned off the lamp and stood for awhile in the dark, letting my eyes adjust to it. Then I went back to the window and pulled the curtain to one side a little, just enough to peer cautiously out. I flinched as I did, half expecting a rock to come through the glass.

Nothing happened. All I saw was an empty lawn, the trees, the distant line of fence and a meadow, dark and still and quiet.

Had I imagined it after all? Had what had happened at Kristy's made me see things in shadows?

No. No, I was sure I'd seen a dark figure, lurking under the tree.

Hadn't I?

I decided not to tell Sharon and my dad, at least not right away. Instead I scooped up Tigger, who was asleep on the bed, and draped him over my shoulder. I walked around the house as casually as I could, making sure all the doors and windows were locked. I told Sharon good night and returned to my room to go to bed.

But it was a long, long time before I fell asleep.

"It was really creepy," I said. "I just happened to look out the window, and there he was!"

"He?" asked Stacey.

"Or she," I said impatiently. "Whoever." I shuddered at the memory.

Stacey asked, "Maybe you should tell your dad and Sharon."

"I know. I probably should." I sighed. Secretly, I was afraid if I told my father that I thought I'd seen someone lurking around our house, he'd start making up a list of strict, new rules "for my own good."

Stacey said, "I can't believe what happened at Kristy's. Talk about creepy."

"Could we *not* talk about creepy right now?" asked Claudia. "That's all we've been talking about. I thought we were here to shop."

"Sorry, Claudia," said Stacey.

Claudia looked contrite. "I'm sorry, too. I didn't mean to be nasty. I guess all this stuff is just psyching me out, you know?"

She turned and refocused her attention on a rack of thin, silky-looking shirts that we'd been examining for at least five minutes. Then she said, "The blue."

"Huh?" I said.

"Try on the blue one," she commanded.

I looked doubtfully at the silky blue shirt. It was a very bright blue. I am not a bright blue sort of person.

On the other hand, Stacey was nodding

slowly. "I can see it," she murmured.

"Okay," I said, "I'll try it on. But I don't promise to like it."

We were shopping at the mall. Specifically, Claudia and Stacey were helping me look for something new (and affordable) for the special football-season-is-over date.

Logan had mentioned the possibility of going to a "real" restaurant for dinner.

He hadn't mentioned sending me any notes.

As if she had read my thoughts, Stacey said, "So, what did Logan say about the note he sent you?"

"He didn't say anything. I don't think he sent it." I'd told everyone in the BSC about the note I'd found in my locker. Everyone except Logan, that is. For some reason, I was waiting for him to say something.

Didn't the fact that he hadn't said anything prove that the note was some kind of weird joke that someone — not Logan — was pulling?

Both Stacey and Claudia thought this made sense.

"Hmm," said Stacey, raising her eyebrows. "I wonder which extremely immature person in SMS might do an extremely childish and stupid thing like sending anonymous notes."

None of us said anything for a moment. But

Mary Anne

I knew we were all thinking of Cokie Mason. Not only had she had a massive crush on Logan, but she also had sent Kristy threatening notes once.

Then Claudia remembered our mission. "The blue shirt," she said, thrusting it into my arms.

We headed for the dressing rooms.

By the time we'd finished shopping, I'd added not a blue shirt but a very thin, lace-edged sweater to my wardrobe. I was going to wear it with a skirt, and one of Stacey's belts. I also bought new, patterned stockings, and Claudia promised to lend me a pair of her earrings "that would be awesome."

I was feeling pretty pleased as we walked out of the mall and headed for the corner, to wait for the bus back to Stoneybrook. We were going back to Claudia's house. Later, Sharon was going to pick up Stacey and me, and drop off Stacey on the way to our house.

Suddenly, I had this creepy sensation. I was sure I was being watched.

I stopped so abruptly that Claudia ran into me. "Hey!" she complained. "Watch out!"

I didn't answer. I turned and looked around the parking lot. Plenty of people were around, driving cars, parking, and walking to and from the mall.

Nobody was paying any attention to me.

That's what I told myself. But I also realized that if someone wanted to, he or she could watch me very easily. He could slump down in the seat of any one of dozens of cars, or crouch down beside or behind one of the cars, in the shadows. There were plenty of ways to see me without being seen.

"Mary Anne?" Claudia touched my shoulder. "Is there a reason you want to wait for the bus in the middle of the road?"

"Oh. Sorry," I said. I felt foolish. I joined Claudia and Stacey in the shelter of a bus stop.

The late afternoon shadows were lengthening. As the days grew colder and winter settled in, the dark came earlier and earlier. It would be almost dark by the time we reached Claudia's.

I shivered.

Claudia said, "I could use some quality junk food about now."

"Claud, we had popcorn in the mall," Stacey reminded her.

"True," Claudia answered regretfully.

I didn't say anything. I just kept looking around. *Someone was watching*. I could feel it. I was sure of it. Someone was out there in one of those cars, watching me.

The way someone had watched my house.

61

But I couldn't prove it. If I said anything, I would probably sound as if I were paranoid, because of what had happened at Kristy's house. And what I thought had happened at mine.

So I kept quiet. And I kept watch, too, until at last the bus arrived and we were able to head safely home.

"We're hooooome," sang Claudia as we pushed open her back door.

From upstairs, I heard a door open, and footsteps.

"De de, de de." Claudia hummed the theme from that old show, *The Twilight Zone*.

Her sister Janine's voice floated down the stairs. "Claudia. You do recollect that it is your responsibility to set the table and start dinner tonight?"

"No sweat," Claudia called back. "Trust me. We'll be feasting before you know it."

Janine didn't answer. Her footsteps retreated along the floor and her door closed.

"What are you making for dinner?" asked Stacey.

"I was thinking of a Twinkie casserole with Dream Whip topping," Claudia answered, deadpan. Then she laughed. "All I have to do is set the table and make the salad, and then help my father cut up some vegetables for the pasta."

"We can help you set the table," I said.

Stacey and I slung our packs over the backs of the kitchen chairs. I put my shopping bag down, and we began to help Claudia set the table for dinner.

We'd just finished folding the napkins when Stacey sniffed the air. "You didn't put something in the oven, or turn on a burner or anything, did you, Claudia?"

"Nope. The frozen meatloaf is tomorrow and it's Janine who has to — " She stopped. She sniffed the air, too.

"Wow," she said. "Something's . . . burning?"

"Maybe someone's burning leaves," I suggested.

"No," said Stacey. "They can't do that anymore. Remember how excited Dawn was when they made it a law that everyone has to put their leaves out for compost for the parks department?"

We sniffed the air again, this time simultaneously.

And we all noticed the same thing at the same time.

The dining room was filling up with smoke.

"Fire?" said Claudia.

Mary Anne

We dropped napkins and silverware on the table and ran back into the kitchen. The smell of burning was much stronger. And the kitchen was filling up with smoke, too.

Claudia yanked the oven door open and Stacey did the same to the microwave. Nothing. I jerked open the pantry door. I saw smoke there, too, but no fire.

Then I saw it. I raised my hand and pointed.

Through the window of the kitchen door, I could see flames leaping up outside.

"Fire!" shouted Claudia. "I'll get Janine."

"I'll call nine-one-one," I said.

Stacey reached for the back door and Claudia said, with amazing calmness, "Don't open the door. It might make the fire worse."

"We should close the kitchen door behind us," I said as Claudia dashed to the foot of the stairs.

"JANINE!" she screamed.

"What?" Janine's voice sound faintly irritated.

"FIRE!" shouted Claudia.

That got Janine's attention. She shot out into the hallway and peered down the stairs.

The smoke was rising now.

She half turned and Claudia said, "Don't go back. Leave now. Come on."

"But my computer — "

"NOW!" shouted Claudia.

We all looked at her in surprise, but Janine obeyed. A moment later, we dashed for the front door, slamming doors behind us as we went. Claudia made a mad dash for the next-door neighbors' to call the fire department, and Stacey and Janine and I ran around to the back of the house.

It was a fire all right. But as hot as it was blazing, it gave me a cold chill.

Because it wasn't an accident. Two trash cans had been set up near the back door. The firefighters said later that rags soaked in gasoline had been stuffed into the cans and then lit, after the cans were set up.

The fire had been set deliberately. And if we hadn't acted as fast as we had, it might have spread — maybe even to the house.

CHAPTER 6

Claudia

Friday

The house still smells like smoak,
sort off. I cant beleieve it hapenned.
Some one set a fire on purpos. Thats
what the firefigters said. Why ?????

"Maybe it's all connected," said Abby.

"How?" Kristy shot back. If I hadn't known better, I'd have thought that all the excitement — if that's what you want to call it — of the last few days was getting on her nerves.

We were halfway through our Friday afternoon meeting of the BSC, but nowhere near through discussing everything that had happened.

Mary Anne said, "Well, first I found that weird note in what looks like Logan's handwriting. But I'm almost absolutely positive he didn't write it. Then, on that very same day, someone throws a rock through your front window and writes graffiti on your front door. I mean, the graffiti was sort of like an anonymous note, too. And then someone sets a fire at Claudia's."

"True," said Kristy. "The police kept asking Watson and Mom if they have any enemies."

"The fire marshal asked us the same question," I said. "They know how it was done, but not a single clue about who did it."

"Same thing at our house," said Kristy. "They're still investigating, but they don't have a single suspect."

"Cokie Mason?" said Stacey.

"No!" cried Mary Anne.

"She's sent anonymous notes before, remember?" Stacey persisted. "And she is jealous of you, Mary Anne."

Mary Anne looked even more unhappy. She always tries to see the best in everyone and I think it shocks her to realize that some people's best sides aren't all that good.

"But what about the fire? I don't know Cokie very well," said Jessi, "but I can't believe that even she would set a fire deliberately."

"I agree," I said. "Or lurk around outside Mary Anne's house in the dark alone. Or throw a rock through a window. Cokie's nasty, but she's not a criminal."

Then Stacey asked, "What about Cary Retlin?"

That stopped us all for a moment. Who could forget Cary Retlin? He'd been involved in a mystery that Stacey had helped solve, when someone had tried to sabotage a school dance. We never had figured out quite how much trouble Cary was capable of making though. He seemed to enjoy it. "Cary Retlin is a possibility," said Mal. She hadn't been talking much, just sitting with her arms folded and a glum, faraway expression on her face. "Or maybe it's just some stranger."

"Some random person?" I asked. I didn't know which was worse: thinking that someone who knew us could be behind the horrible, creepy things that had been happening, or that some stranger might be stalking us and our families.

Suddenly I didn't want to talk about it anymore. The police and the fire marshal were on the case. They could handle it. No need for us to worry.

But it didn't look as though we were going to be cut loose from crime anytime soon. Abby said, "Well, solve *this* mystery, then. Why haven't we heard anything about that burglary Kristy and I saw on Wednesday? Nothing in the newspapers, nothing on television, *nada*. Total *nada*."

Jessi suggested, "Maybe there was more important news?"

"Hey, I wasn't expecting a headline," said Abby, "but it should have at least made the police blotter section."

"You read the police reports in the newspaper?" Mary Anne said, her eyes widening.

"Sure. Doesn't everybody?" asked Abby.

Kristy said, "Maybe it wouldn't be a bad idea to check it out now. We could see if anything like what's been happening to us has been happening around Stoneybrook. Maybe it's part of some vandalism wave or something."

I'm not a coward, but I was shaken by what had happened. The assumption that the events could be linked together somehow, that a single person could be responsible for so much evil, made the smell of smoke that lingered in the air seem positively malevolent.

The only real damage had been to our trash cans, but I knew it could have been worse.

Much worse.

What if we hadn't come home when we did? What if Janine hadn't smelled the smoke until . . .

"My mom and dad get the newspaper," I said brightly. I jumped up and ran out of the room and downstairs to the front door.

The newspaper had been delivered. I bent to pick it up — then slowly straightened.

What if someone were out there, right now, watching my house?

Quickly I slammed the door and ran back upstairs, dropping the newspaper on Kristy's lap as I returned to my seat.

"Let me see some of it," said Abby.

Kristy handed her a section of the newspaper without speaking.

"Anybody else want part of the paper?" asked Abby, looking around.

"Here it is," said Kristy. " 'Local Crime

Beat.' Look, Claudia! We're in it!"

Clearing her throat, Kristy read the crime report aloud.

The fire at our house was described as "Fire of Mysterious Origin." That meant, after we'd deciphered the weird language the police report was written in, that there'd been a fire and nobody knew who had set it. "Arson suspected," the report concluded.

Arson. The word sent a chill down my spine.

I looked around the room and realized that I wasn't the only one who had been affected by the word. *Arson*. It had a nasty, criminal sound to it. But then, why shouldn't it? It was the name of a crime.

"Are you going to keep reading?" Abby asked. "If it's too much, I'll — "

"It's fine," said Kristy. She kept reading. Whoever had broken the window and sprayed the threat on her front door was described as a "vandal." No suspects, the report said.

"Well, great." Abby sounded disgusted. "Why haven't they reported the burglary?"

"Maybe you just missed seeing it," suggested Jessi.

"Nope," said Abby.

The phone rang and for a moment we all

stared at it as if we didn't know why it was making that noise. Then Stacey said, "Oh!" and picked it up.

We went on with business as usual after that. Kristy checked the weather report in the paper, and read a prediction of "possible snow" for the weekend at Shadow Lake.

She groaned.

"Don't they have snow machines at the ski areas?" I asked.

"It's not the same," Kristy complained.

"You are so right," agreed Abby. "Nothing like real powder."

Stacey suddenly laughed. "As long as it's soft! I'm barely off the bunny slope, don't forget."

I opened my mouth to tell Stacey not to worry, that I'd stick with her. But I didn't have a chance.

"Hey, no prob," said Abby. "I'll have you skiing the black diamond trails in no time."

"Black diamond? Oh, right. The really hard ones." Stacey laughed again. "That'll be the day."

"Well, maybe not the expert trails," Abby conceded.

She sounded so sure of herself.

So cocky.

Aloud I said, "You know, people get killed

every year, trying to ski on trails they aren't ready for. Killed *dead*."

Abby looked startled. And she wasn't the only one.

I folded my arms. "I mean, I don't want to see Stacey getting hurt. She doesn't have to prove anything. She just wants to have a good time."

Mary Anne the peacemaker intervened. "Well, you'll have a good time no matter what kind of snow you have. And wait until you see Shadow Lake, Abby. It's really, really beautiful."

"Yeah," said Kristy. She leaned back in her chair and pushed her visor up. "Shadow Lake. I can hardly wait."

She looked at her watch. "This meeting . . ."

But before she could adjourn, the phone rang one last time.

I picked it up. "Baby-sitters Club. May I help you?" I asked.

No one answered.

"Hello?" I said.

Again no one answered.

"Hello!" I almost shouted.

"You're next," a voice whispered.

And then the line went dead.

CHAPTER 7

Kristy

Sunday

It was not the best weekend of my life. I tried to concentrate on important things, like waxing my skis and getting my gear ready for Shadow Lake. (And, okay, my homework.) But its hard to concentrate when every ring of the phone makes you jump. Or when going outside makes you nervous. I kept looking over my shoulder, thinking that someone was following me. And I wasn't the only one who was having a bad weekend.

Mary Anne's voice said, "He just called again."

"He, who?" I asked. "Logan?"

Of course, by then, I knew it wasn't Logan. Because the BSC was getting swamped with crank calls. Not heavy breathing calls. Just frightening, horrible silences. The silences of someone listening on the other end of the phone, and enjoying the panic in your voice as you say, "Hello. Hello? *Hello! WHO'S THERE?*" before slamming the phone down, good and hard.

We'd dealt with phantom phone calls before, Claudia in particular. They hadn't been as creepy as these.

"Listen," I said, "From now on, we should all ring once and then call right back. That way we'll know it's not the anonymous phone caller."

Mary Anne said, "My father got a phone call from someone asking for a Mr. Smith. Doesn't that sound fake to you? Do you think it was the guy who's been calling us?"

"Maybe. Maybe not. Most of my phone calls have been when I'm the only one here, or the oldest one here," I said.

"As if he *knows*," Mary Anne said, almost tearfully. "As if he's *watching*."

"Let him watch. There's nothing he can do."
But I knew that wasn't true. He — or she —
whoever it was, had done plenty already.

Stacey and Claudia reported the same pat-
tern: hang-up phone calls when they answered the phone. Usually the calls came
when they were home alone, or hanging out
together, or at least when no adults were
around who were more likely to answer the
phone. I'd taken to turning on the answering
machine when I was home and screening all
the incoming calls. So had Stacey. But although Claudia has an answering machine for
her phone, the Kishis don't have one for the
family phone, and the Spiers use an answering
service that's only in effect during the work-
days, when they aren't home and Mary Anne
is at school.

The phone calls had been going on all weekend. But so far, Mal, Jessi, and Abby hadn't
gotten any. But then, Jessi's dad and Mal's
parents had been home all weekend, while
Abby and Anna and their mom practically
hadn't been home at all.

Then, abruptly, the calls stopped. Not a single random ring after the phone call to Mary
Anne on Sunday afternoon.

I still gave the phone a dark, suspicious look

every time it rang, though. And I still turned the answering machine on when I was home alone.

Whoever it was might have just taken the night off.

I also kept a close eye on the newspaper, to see if there had been any news about the burglary. So did Abby.

Neither of us had seen a word about a house being burglarized.

On Monday before school, I decided that no news was *not* good news. I called Sergeant Johnson to ask him if the burglars had been caught.

"No," he said slowly. "No, no suspects have been apprehended." He paused, then said, "We don't have a complainant."

"What do you mean? I'm complaining! Someone broke into someone's house!"

"Ms. Thomas . . ."

"Call me Kristy."

"Kristy. When we contacted the owner of the house, Mr. . . ." Sergeant Johnson paused, and I could hear the rustling of paper. "Mr. H. Joseph Seger, he said that the window was broken the previous night when he was pruning a tree and miscalculated the fall of a large branch."

"Prune? Did he say 'prune'?" I asked.

The paper rustled again. "Yes. That was his word."

"Ha!" I said. "No one prunes trees this time of year!" (Not for nothing am I the stepdaughter of Watson Brewer, and the granddaughter of Nannie, both master gardeners, and between them the owners of the largest collection of gardening books in the universe.)

Sergeant Johnson said, "Hmmm."

Of course, Mr. H. Joseph Seger could have just been a bad gardener. It was possible.

But it didn't make sense.

"We *did* hear glass breaking. We *did* see someone run by, wearing a stocking mask and carrying a gym bag. Abby and I both did. Why would we make something like that up?"

Another pause. Then Sergeant Johnson said, "I don't doubt what you say. But there is nothing we can do if Mr. Seger says there was no crime."

"Oh," I said. "So that's it, then?"

"Unless something changes," said Sergeant Johnson. "If it does, we'll be in touch."

"Thank you," I said, and hung up. I tried to remember whether I'd seen any tree branches lying around in the broken glass that afternoon. But I couldn't. Besides, Mr. Seger would just say that he'd already cleared the branch away.

But why clear away a branch and not the broken glass? Why lie about the incident in the first place?

"Kristy!" Watson called. "Your bus is here."

I grabbed my pack and headed for school.

Abby said sarcastically, "Well, if he wasn't a burglar, who *was* the guy in the mask who ran past us? The housekeeper, taking out the garbage?"

I expected steam to start pouring out of Abby's ears at any moment.

Fortunately, Mary Anne sat down at that moment. "Garbage?" she said, giving me a reproving frown. "Are you making gross jokes about the food, too, Abby? Because if you and Kristy are both going to — "

Abby looked startled. I couldn't help but grin. "We're not making food jokes," I assured her. "We're talking about the burglar."

We were eating lunch in the cafeteria at SMS together, as we usually did: Stacey, Claudia, Mary Anne, Abby, and me. Sometimes Logan joins us, but I didn't see him around today. Jessi and Mal don't sit with us, because the sixth-graders have a different lunch period.

As Mary Anne gave her own lunch a less than approving look I filled her in on my conversation with Sergeant Johnson that morning.

"Why would Mr. Seger lie about someone breaking into his house?" asked Mary Anne.

"Because he's hiding something, of course," said Abby impatiently.

Everybody was quiet for a moment. I gave my green Jell-O a poke and watched it wiggle.

"Maybe he has something inside the house he doesn't want the police to see," Claudia suggested. "Like . . . like stolen art."

"Or counterfeit money," said Stacey.

Since she and Claud had both been seriously involved in mysteries involving, respectively, counterfeit money and stolen art, these suggestions were not as farfetched as they might seem. As we all knew, it could happen in Stoneybrook. It already had.

"Maybe," I said slowly.

"He's hiding something," said Abby. "What it is isn't important right now. What's more important is, are the burglars connected to all this — I mean, to the bizzaro, sicko things that have been happening to us?"

I said, "You and I were wearing nametags, Abby. He could have seen those, remembered

80

our names, and tracked us down that way. But how does he know we're connected to the rest of the BSC?"

Mary Anne said, "Maybe he picked up one of our fliers and saw your name?"

"It's possible," I said. "But pretty remote. We haven't given those out in awhile."

"He followed us that night?" suggested Abby and then immediately answered her own question. "No. If you're running from the scene of a crime, you don't stop to follow someone home."

"No, it doesn't make sense, does it?" Stacey sighed. She finished the last of her apple and stood up. "I've got to book," she said. "See you later."

"I guess we have a mystery on our hands," said Claudia. She didn't sound all that unhappy at the prospect.

"It's possible," I said. I gave the green Jell-O on my plate another poke. It quivered in what I can only describe as a suspicious manner. Was it alive? Was it a slimy oyster in a green disguise? "But the only mystery right now is how this Jell-O could . . ."

I looked up and caught Mary Anne's eye. She gave me what was, for her, a warning glare.

"Never mind," I said quickly.

I ate my Jell-O.

Business was brisk that afternoon at the BSC meeting. Five minutes after I'd called the meeting to order, we'd taken three phone calls.

None of them anonymous. None of them hang-ups. All of them from clients we knew.

"I'm not sure I'd want to take a job with a new client right now," Claudia observed thoughtfully, when I pointed out this important fact. "I mean, the phone calls *seem* to have stopped. But maybe whoever it is, is just planning something worse."

Jessi's eyes widened. "Worse?" she repeated. "Worse how?"

"Wow, Claudia, you're right!" Abby exclaimed. "He calls us up, he pretends he wants a baby-sitter. He gives us a false address, we go there. It's a dark and stormy night. The door opens. We go inside and . . . *eeeeek!*"

We all jumped about a hundred feet into the air. Claudia threw up her hands and popcorn sprayed all over her room.

Abby, who'd been sitting on the floor, fell back against the side of Claudia's bed laughing. "Gotcha!" she cried.

The phone rang. I picked it up, fixing Abby

(who alone was still laughing) with a Look. It was Mrs. Arnold, requesting a sitter for her twins, Carolyn and Marilyn. I took the call without saying any names then hung up the phone. I caught Mary Anne's eye, stared hard at her, then winked very, very slightly.

"It's a new client," I announced.

Claudia froze in the act of picking up the popcorn. A hush fell over the room. Abby even stopped laughing.

"Are you *serious*?" Abby asked.

I nodded. "Friday night. At a house on Elm Street." I kept staring at Mary Anne. "What does the appointment book look like for Friday night?"

Mary Anne flipped open her book. She ran her finger down the page. "Jessi — no, it's at night. I can't, I have a date." She lifted her eyes from the page. "Abby, you're the only one who is free. Can you do it?"

"Ah, well, ah . . ." Abby looked wildly around the room. "But, uh — *Elm* Street?"

I couldn't keep it together any longer. I cracked up. "Gotcha back!" I said.

Another moment of silence and then everyone began to hoot.

"Good one!" said Claudia.

"Excellent acting, Mary Anne," put in Mal.

Abby, her face red, said, "Okay, okay. I owe

you one, Kristy Thomas and Mary Anne Spier."

When we'd settled down (and laughed off some of the tension that had been building up), we set up the baby-sitting job for Mrs. Arnold (for Tuesday afternoon, which Mal took). Then Jessi said, "I have some new business, sort of."

"Okay," I said.

"It's Becca. She told me she's seen a man with a blue tattoo around Stoneybrook."

"A blue tattoo!" Stacey exclaimed. "What kind of tattoo? What did he look like? Remember, that counterfeiter we helped catch? I think he had a blue tattoo. I can't remember where."

Jessi shrugged. "I thought that guy went to prison for counterfeiting."

"It's in the notebook somewhere," murmured Mary Anne.

Claudia picked up the club notebook from her desk and handed it to Stacey. Stacey made a face. "Great," she said. "I have to go through all this to look up the blue tattoo? I spend enough time with this notebook writing up my sitting jobs. Bummer."

She gave a big, theatrical sigh and plopped the notebook open on her lap (she was sitting cross-legged on Claudia's bed) and began to rifle through the pages.

I looked at the notebook. It was pretty thick. In fact, it looked like the notes from a thousand classes at school. It was easy enough to look up past sitting jobs; all we had to do was check out the date in Mary Anne's appointment book and then look up that date in the notebook, since all the entries have dates at the top. But there was no way of looking up specific things, no index, no table of contents. Too bad we hadn't kept a separate mystery notebook, I thought.

This shows how rattled I was by the mystery. I had this stupendous, brilliant idea and I didn't even realize it right away. I just sat there in my chair, frowning, watching Stacey go through the notebook.

It actually took me a whole minute before I shouted, *"That's it!"*

Everyone jumped again. Clearly this mystery was getting on our nerves.

"Will you stop that?" Claudia complained.

"Sorry," I said. "But listen. Why don't we keep a mystery notebook? I mean, we have enough material for a separate book. And then we could look things up in it, and use it to help solve cases as we go along."

85

"*Cases?* You think we're going to be solving lots more mysteries?" teased Mary Anne.

"The way things are going, it could happen," I said.

"True." Mal looked thoughtful. "I think it's a great idea."

"Just one problem," Claudia pointed out. "Who's going to go through the notebook and put all the old mysteries together? I don't volunteer."

"Me either," said Abby.

Mal said, "I will. Volunteer, I mean. It sounds like fun."

"Sounds like a book report," said Claudia. Then another thought struck her. "Oh, no! We'll have to write in *another* notebook!"

The phone rang twice more. We set up two more jobs — with regular clients. Then the meeting was over.

Stacey handed the BSC notebook to Mal. After making a careful note, she also gave Mal some money. "For the mystery notebook," she said.

"Thanks," said Mal. "I'll let you know when I find the stuff about the man with the blue tattoo."

"We have to begin investigating right away," I said. "Like tomorrow. Tuesday. Morning."

"We get the point, Kristy," said Mal. "I'll buy the notebook tomorrow."

"Because we're leaving for Shadow Lake at the end of the week, don't forget." I stood up and put on my jacket and picked up my pack. "And guess what? A *huge* snowstorm is supposed to be coming. I just hope it hits Shadow Lake the same time we do. It's about time we had some good luck."

Famous last words.

CHAPTER 8

Shannon

Tuesday

Kristy Thomas, PI and WOA (Private
Investigator and Woman of Action) called
me last night to tell me about this notebook
and the investigation into the mystery (or
mysteries) haunting the BSC. She enlisted
me, along with Abby and Claudia, to go to the
Stoneybrook Public Library to do some investigating. Usually, background work is the dull
part of an investigation. But today I
discovered that research can be pretty
exciting. And scary...

"Shannon."

"Hi, Kristy. What's up?" I asked.

"Can you go to the library with some of us tomorrow?"

"Sure," I said. Then I remembered to ask, "What for?"

Kristy told me about Mr. Seger and his mysterious burglary. She also told me about the mystery notebook.

"It's a fact-gathering mission," she said. "We're looking for information."

"Also known as clues?" I suggested.

"Of course," said Kristy. "We're going to put everything we learn into our notebook and see what we come up with."

"See how things add up. See what 'x' is in the equation," I said.

"Have you been talking to Stacey already?" asked Kristy.

"No," I answered, trying not to laugh. Kristy can be pretty intense sometimes. But then, scary things had been happening to the BSC — and they would be even scarier if they were tied together.

Maybe that's why I wanted to laugh — I was scared. Sometimes being scared affects people that way.

We made plans to meet.

Shannon

* * *

The next afternoon, Kristy, Claudia, and Abby were waiting for me on the front steps of the Stoneybrook Public Library.

"Mal's on a stakeout," said Kristy. "We're going to take separate notes and incorporate them into the mystery notebook as soon as she's brought it up to date."

"Stakeout?" I said.

"Sitting at the Rodowskys'. Keeping an eye on the Seger residence," Kristy explained in what sounded suspiciously like police-ese.

"Okay, okay," I said. "Lead on, Sherlock."

"Agatha," said Abby. "Agatha Kristy. Get it?"

We all groaned and went inside.

Where does Abby get her awful puns?

As we passed the desk, Abby whispered, "Okay, spread out and try to act normal." She waved to Mrs. Kishi and gave her a big grin. "Hi!" she said. "Read any good books lately?"

Claudia said, "You are so *weird*. And my mom's heard that line about a thousand times." She waved to her mom, too, and shrugged her shoulders. Mrs. Kishi gave us a puzzled smile and we walked toward the computer catalogue.

"How do you look someone up in the library?" Kristy asked. "Apart from the phone book, I mean."

Claudia said, "You can look in the Stoney-brook *Who's Who*. Also the news index of the newspaper."

"Wow. Okay." Kristy nodded approvingly. "Let's start with the *Who's Who*."

"How did you know that, anyway?" Abby asked Claudia.

"My mother is a librarian and my sister is a genius," Claudia replied. "I know these things." She grinned. "Besides, I asked Janine last night."

"Did you tell her what was going on?" asked Kristy.

"No." Claudia grinned again. "You know Janine. She likes knowing the answers to questions. So I asked her a bunch of questions and this was just one of them."

"Sneaky. Devious. Excellent," said Kristy. She turned and stopped again. "Where is the Stoneybrook *Who's Who*?"

"That I didn't ask her," Claudia admitted.

"I'll go ask at the desk," I volunteered. "If your mom has any questions, I can just say I'm doing research and she'll think it's for my homework."

But Mrs. Kishi didn't ask any questions. She

just smiled and said hello and asked me how I was doing, and then told me where to find what we were looking for.

A few minutes later we'd staked out a table in the corner of the library, with our backs to the wall (at Kristy's insistence).

"Here it is," said Abby. "Mr. Seger. He's a member of the Stoneybrook Business Bureau — that sounds pretty respectable — his wife is deceased, and he has one son who is in high school, going by his date of birth."

"What's his son's name?" asked Claudia.

"Noah." Abby looked from Claudia to Kristy. "Do you think he's in high school here? Do you think your sister or your brothers would know him?"

Both Kristy and Claudia shrugged. Then Kristy asked, "Is that all?"

"That's it." I said. I was disappointed. The *Who's Who* didn't have very much what's what, in my humble opinion.

"Yeah." Abby sounded disappointed, too.

"Let's photocopy it," said Kristy. "There could be a clue there."

Abby picked up the book. Pretending to stagger slightly under its weight, she turned toward the photocopy room. "Anybody have change?" she asked.

We pooled our change and Abby, still in her

fake stagger mode, lurched away.

A few minutes later she came lurching back.

"Ha, ha . . ." Kristy began. Her voice trailed off.

Abby's face was a ghastly greenish-white.

"What's wrong?" I asked, jumping up from the table. Abby dropped the *Who's Who* with a thump. She also dropped several photocopies of the page about Mr. Seger.

And one photocopy, very crooked but quite clear, of a photograph of Kristy, Mary Anne, Claudia, Stacey, and Dawn.

"Where did you find this?" demanded Kristy.

Abby sat down in the chair. Color was returning to her face. Her voice sounded normal, but abnormally serious, for her. "It was just sitting there, staring up at me from the recycle bin."

"Right on top?" I asked.

"Well, not right on top." Abby looked a little sheepish. "I was sort of going through it while the machine was making copies. You know, checking out what other people make copies of. Anyway, there it was, just underneath the first few pieces of paper. It was creepy. I mean, it freaked me out."

"It's the photo that was taken of us when we solved that pet-napping mystery, with

Dawn," said Kristy. "The one that was in the *Stoneybrook News*. Remember? Jessi and Mal were on the ends and got cropped out and were majorly annoyed."

"That's where the burglar found our names!" Claudia exclaimed. "He must have looked up 'Kristy Thomas' in the news index and found our picture in the paper. That's why all the phone calls and weird stuff have been happening to just the four of us, unless Dawn, all the way out in California — "

"Mary Anne talked to Dawn on Sunday and told her what was going on," said Kristy. "Dawn would have told Mary Anne then if she'd been getting weird phone calls or anything, and she didn't."

"Talk about major clues," said Abby. "I mean, this proves that the burglars must be behind the vandalism, right? They saw your name, Kristy, and mine, and looked us both up in the newspaper index and since I'm not famous all over town — yet — they found you. Wow. I bet Jessi and Mal are going to be glad they got cropped out of the photo now!"

"It could be." Kristy had picked up the photocopies of the information about Mr. Seger and handed them around to each of us before tucking the extra ones in her notebook.

"Someone could have looked up any one of

the five names in the newspaper index," I pointed out. "Not that I believe that. What I believe is that your burglar did get Kristy's name from her tag."

"That means he was here, in this library, not too long ago. Too bad we can't find out who made copies," Abby said regretfully. Then she brightened. "You think he's still here?"

"No!" said Claudia so firmly we all jumped.

We looked quickly and nervously around. But nobody sinister was lurking nearby. Or if they were, they were cleverly disguised as a teenaged boy helping his kid sister with her homework, two older women thumbing through a towering stack of financial reports, and someone who looked like a college student staring glumly down at an open book without turning a page.

"Let's check out Mr. Seger in the *Stoneybrook News* index," suggested Kristy.

Claudia put the *Who's Who* back on the shelf, and we went to the computers. We scrolled through the index twice, but Mr. Seger wasn't as famous as the Baby-sitters Club. He'd never made the news, at least not according to the index.

"Or not under the name he's using now," said Abby darkly.

Shannon

We looked at her. "Well, maybe it is a fake name," she said. "You never know."

It was time to go. We'd done all the investigating we could do for one day. We trudged out of the library silently. Abby even forgot to goof on Mrs. Kishi as we passed the front desk on the way to the door.

"Find everything you need?" asked Mrs. Kishi.

"Yes, thank you," Kristy answered. "Plenty."

"Yeah," I added under my breath. "We found out how much we don't know."

CHAPTER 9

Mallory

Tuesday

When you have red hair and glasses, it isn't easy to blend in with the scenery. I know this from experience. I am often the only kid with red hair in a classroom — and often the first one called on. It is not a coincidence.

But that is another mystery. In this mystery, we were going on a stakeout. Assignment: Seger. So I went undercover in the ultimate disguise: baby-sitter.

Mallory
ʕ•ᴥ•ʔ

Have you ever noticed how when you are
with kids, people remember you as a unit, like
"a bunch of kids" or "a girl with two little kids
(or three or four)"?

Anyway, I was sitting for the Rodowskys
on Tuesday afternoon — and I was staking
out Mr. Seger's house next door. The Rodowskys' kitchen was on the side of the house
that was next to Mr. Seger's house, so naturally I'd decided we should do some kitchen-
related activities.

All three Rodowsky boys were enthusiastic
about this idea. It was only after I'd suggested
it that I began to have second thoughts.

A kitchen is filled with potential for disas-
ters. And Jackie Rodowsky, age seven, is
known, among the members of the BSC, as
the Walking Disaster.

Trouble follows him wherever he goes —
except when he is walking into it head-on.
Jackie is used to it. But it is *extremely* hard on
other people if they are not used to it.

Since I have four brothers, three of whom
are triplets, I am used to chaos and catastrophe. In fact, when I write the first volume of
my autobiography, I am going to call it *Chaos
and Catastrophe*. Or maybe that will be the title
of the opening chapter. . . .

That day we decided to make cookies. (But Shea, who is nine, and Jackie weren't calling them cookies. They were calling them Edible Slammers, after their Pogs and Slammers games, and so was Archie, who is four and copies everything his two older brothers do, even when he isn't sure why they are doing it.)

Of course I spent some time checking out the house next door from the kitchen window. The glass had been cleaned up. The window had been replaced. Not surprisingly, no tree branch was in sight.

In fact, the only tree of any size near the house wasn't near enough for one of its branches to fall through that window, unless the tree was bent toward it at a forty-five degree angle.

Shea said, "Jackie, if you put chocolate chips up your nose . . ."

I spun around. "Don't you dare!"

Jackie grinned at me. "I wasn't really going to," he said. "I just said it would make a really excellent gross joke."

Great, I thought. Wait till Kristy hears about this. Something else to add to her gross food jokes at lunch. I'd heard *plenty* about her lunchroom jokes, enough to make me almost glad the sixth-graders have a different lunch period than the eighth-graders. I could hear Kristy now: "Hey, you guys, you know where they *keep* these chocolate chips?"

I saw that Archie was looking extremely interested in the idea and quickly moved the chocolate chips out of his reach to the middle of the table. I safety-pinned a large, clean, blue and white dishtowel to Archie's shirt for an apron, and Shea and Jackie put on old aprons. Jackie chose a bright pink apron, which looked startling, to say the least, with his hair. Shea opted for a flaming red one that said "BARBECUE ON, DUDES." His color combination was pretty eye-catching, too.

I settled on your basic navy blue apron — a nice, conservative choice that doesn't show spots.

Tying on my apron, I took another quick glance out the window, noted that no one seemed to be home, then turned back to the cookies.

Although members of the BSC have, at times, made very exotic cookies, we stuck to basics that afternoon. We made Tollhouse cookies and plain oatmeal raisin cookies (excuse me, Slammers).

After we put them in the oven, I made a game out of cleaning up the kitchen. The only disaster was when Jackie knocked over a chair with his enthusiastic sweeping. This would not have been a disaster at all, except that the chair somehow hit the trashcan, which tipped over and spilled garbage across the kitchen floor, and hit Bo's dog dishes, splattering dog food and water everywhere.

"Uh-oh," said Jackie.

Archie laughed delightedly. "A mess!" he proclaimed.

Bo, who had heard the commotion and naturally came to investigate the sound of his food bowl rattling, joined in, barking and doing a happy dog dance in the mess.

We went into action automatically (the Rodowsky boys know everything there is to know about cleaning) and we soon had the mess cleaned up — somewhat, I suspect, to the disappointment of Archie and Bo.

The stove timer went off and Jackie shouted, "The Slammers!" and lunged for the oven door.

I lunged for Jackie just as he pulled the oven door open. Steam billowed up and fogged my glasses.

"Hey!" I said and Jackie let the oven door slam shut.

A pot fell off the stove onto my toe. Fortunately, it was empty.

"Sorry," said Jackie.

"It's okay. No problem," I said, taking off my glasses to wipe them and squint at him. "But why don't you let Shea take the cookies out of the oven — with an oven mitt, Shea — and put them on top of the stove. When they're cool, all three of you can help put them in the cookie jar."

Archie picked up the pot and handed it to me.

"Thank you, Archie," I said.

"Welcome," he replied.

A movement caught my eye. I dashed to the kitchen window and squinted out. Then I realized I wasn't wearing my glasses and put them on.

A short kid (at least, he looked short to me) with brown hair and a baseball cap, and a gray pack slung over one shoulder, was standing at the side door of the Segers' house. He was wearing black sneakers, faded jeans, and an old leather bomber jacket.

I caught my breath. A burglar?

Then, when the kid took a key out of his pocket and opened the door, I realized that he must live there. Did Mr. Seger have a son? I wondered.

"Excuse me," I said to the Rodowsky boys. I dashed to my backpack, whipped out my mystery notebook, and wrote a description of the kid on the blank page under "Stakeout: Seger Burglary." I also wrote in the time he'd arrived home, and what I had noticed about the house (no glass, no tree within glass-breaking distance).

As far as I could tell, the kid stayed in for the rest of the afternoon. Mr. Seger hadn't come home when I left the Rodowskys.

And the only other disaster was when Jackie slammed the door on his finger and it fell in crumbs to the floor. As you might have guessed, "it" wasn't his finger, it was the cookie he was holding.

So it didn't scare me too much.

Jackie just laughed. "Cool," he said. "Slammers."

As I walked my bicycle to the sidewalk on the other side of the street, someone came jogging toward me. It was Abby.

"Hi," I said, surprised.

"Hi. I'm here to relieve you," she said.

"Relieve me?"

"On the stakeout," she explained.

"Oh." I looked around. "Don't you have to get home for dinner?"

Abby shrugged. "I'm on my way home from Claudia's." Abby filled me in on what had happened. "Anna knows where I am," she

103

concluded. "So it's okay. Besides, I'm not going to stay out here freezing for that long. I'm just going to jog around the block for awhile, so I don't look suspicious."

Before Abby could put her plan into effect, however, a car pulled into Mr. Seger's driveway.

Abby whipped out a tiny notebook and wrote something down.

"What're you doing?" I whispered (although there was no chance whoever it was could hear me all the way across the street).

"License plate," she whispered back, "and car description. And description of the guy."

"Is he Mr. Seger?"

"Maybe," she said.

We both watched as a short man got out of the car. He was wearing a brown suit and his brown hair was combed to one side the way men sometimes comb their hair to hide bald spots. He seemed pretty ordinary.

"Look," I said. "He has two stickers on the back of his car."

"Can you see what they say?"

I shook my head. It was getting dark.

Mr. Seger let himself in the side door of the house, confirming his identity. The light in the kitchen of his house (at least, I assumed it was the kitchen) went on.

Abby jogged forward.

"Where are you going?" I asked in alarm.

She didn't answer. A moment later I saw her crouch by the back bumper of the car and write furiously in her notebook.

Then she jogged back to me. "Stoneybrook Business Bureau stickers," she reported. "The blue hexagon is last year's and the orange one is for this year. . . . Well, I better keep moving. Don't want to look suspicious. See ya later, Mal."

Abby jogged away.

I climbed on my bicycle in a daze and pedaled home.

When I got home, my parents were talking about insulation. I felt that this was becoming an unhealthy obsession with them. But I didn't mention it, although my mother did say, as I walked by the door of the den, "Mallory? Was that jacket warm enough for the weather today?"

See what I mean?

"The Stoneybrook Business Bureau," said Kristy. "All roads seem to point to it."

It was the next afternoon. We'd convened a special meeting of the BSC on the steps of the school to "review the case" as Kristy put it. Among us, we'd managed to keep Mr. Se-

105

ger's house pretty well staked out, except during the night. Kristy and Abby had gone out for an early morning jog that just happened to take them by Mr. Seger's house. ("We split up at the corner and took turns circling the block," Abby explained.) When they'd had to go home to get ready for school, Stacey had taken over the watch, standing at the bus stop at the end of the road and sauntering casually along the street.

There had been additional sightings of Noah and of Mr. Seger: Noah climbing into the car with Mr. Seger that morning before school, Noah looking glum and Mr. Seger looking tense. Noah had returned shortly after that and gone in the house. He hadn't emerged by the time Stacey had to leave for school.

Nobody had seen the Ford Escort.

Stacey, meanwhile, told us she'd give us a "full report" at the BSC meeting, then headed out to baby-sit the Rodowskys again. Claudia, who was heading home to start work on a report, walked with her. Abby had soccer practice, so that left Mary Anne, Jessi, Kristy, and me.

We headed for the Stoneybrook Business Bureau. It turned out to be an old house in the middle of Stoneybrook that had been turned into an office building, along with most of the other houses on the street. We passed a dentist, a lawyer, a secondhand clothing store, and a used bookstore, before we reached the house we were looking for, a white building with red trim.

We opened the door and went in. Just to the right of the front hall was a room where a secretary sat behind a desk. He nodded at us.

Kristy said, "Hello," and walked in.

"Hello," said the secretary, smiling. "What can I do for you?"

"Well, we're doing a report for school," said Kristy. "Or at least, I am. About small businesses in Stoneybrook. And I, ah, wanted to interview some of the members of the bureau."

"Sounds like a good idea," said the secretary. "Let me get you our membership list."

"You have a list?" I asked, surprised. "I mean, one that we can look at?"

"Better than that, I'll make you a copy," said the secretary. He took a file out of one of his lower desk drawers. "If you'll excuse me for a moment, I'll be right back with this."

"Wow," Jessi said softly after he'd left. "That was easy."

The secretary returned and handed Kristy four sheets of paper stapled together. "Here's the list of our member businesses."

"Thanks," said Kristy, folding it carefully and putting it in her pack.

"Let us know if we can be of any further help," said the secretary. "And good luck with that report."

"Thanks," Kristy replied. We turned and walked casually toward the door. We had almost reached it when the secretary cried, "Stop!"

I froze.

Kristy turned.

The secretary hurried toward her with another set of sheets. "I'm sorry," he said. "I gave you last year's list. Here's one that is more up-to-date. I have extra copies of this one on hand."

"Oh," said Kristy. "Do you mind if I keep both lists?"

"Be my guest," said the secretary. The phone began to ring and he hurried back to his desk.

Later, at the BSC meeting, Stacey reported that Mr. Seger had come home early that afternoon, while she was sitting for the Rodowskys, then left. Noah, who obviously had left the house after Stacey had gone to school, had come home and gone inside, slamming the door. Mr. Seger had then returned and gone inside. The two had emerged a short time later. They'd left, in Mr. Seger's car, and hadn't returned by the time the Rodowskys had come home.

"You know, for only two people, they come and go almost as much as my whole family," I commented.

Kristy studied the list, then handed it around. "Mr. Seger's there on both lists, a member in good standing," she said. "But it doesn't say what he does. It just says, 'Seger Associates.' "

"Whatever he does, he keeps his own hours. And if the business is named after him, he must be the boss," said Stacey.

"Maybe he's an embezzler!" Claudia exclaimed. "Maybe he has stacks and stacks of embezzled money around his house and that's why he didn't want the police to come in. And maybe that's why he can't report it stolen — because he stole it first!"

We all liked that idea. It seemed to make sense.

But would Mr. Seger embezzle money from his own business? And why?

Mallory
☺

I sighed. I settled back on the floor by the corner of Claudia's bed and ate some chips. We had a lot more clues.

And the mystery was more mysterious than ever.

CHAPTER 10

Stacey

Think snow? Who had time to think at all? The last two days before we left for Shadow Lake went by like an express subway train: a big roar and a lot of voices, talking at the tops of their lungs. And while we were accumulating clues, whoever was stalking the BSC was coming closer and closer. Too close.

Dangerously close.

"Hello?" I said.

"You're next," a voice whispered.

I slammed down the phone.

My hands started to shake. With trembling fingers I picked up the phone and called Claudia's house.

Call me absentminded. Call me a space cadet. I'd actually forgotten about the hang-up phone calls. With two days to go before we left for Shadow Lake, I'd had a lot on my mind.

Such as what to wear. And how to act with Sam. And whether it would snow. I've only been skiing a couple of times, but I couldn't wait to get out there on the bunny slopes again. I was psyched for the trip. In fact, I was staring at my clothes — which were spread out on my bed and on the chair in my room — making very important clothing decisions when he (or she) called.

I forgot about my clothes as I listened to the phone ring. Then I thought suddenly, what if Claudia is there by herself? What if *he's* got her? What if she's tied up at this very moment, sitting there helplessly, listening to the phone . . .

"Hello?" Claud answered in a very un-Claudlike, cautious way.

"He's back," I gasped. "He called me. And he spoke again."

"He said, 'You're next.' Right?"

"How did you know?" I said. I heard my voice go up and thought, Get a grip, McGill. Then I said, "He's called you, too!"

"Yup. We're part of his little phone terrorist circle."

I said, "Maybe it *is* Cokie. Or Cary. I mean, maybe they heard about the graffiti on Kristy's door and they're calling us to freak us out."

"Maybe. But I don't think so." Claudia sighed. "What do we do?"

"Answer the phone very, very carefully," I said. Then I added, "I'm going to call Kristy and let her know."

"I'll call Mary Anne," said Claudia.

"Good," I said. "And call me back if anything else happens."

"Don't worry, I will," said Claudia fervently.

Kristy took the news calmly. She said, "I'll check and see if anyone else has gotten phone calls. But I think it is just limited to the four of us, because whoever it is found our names in that newspaper article."

"Are you home alone?" I asked.

"Nah," said Kristy. "Nannie's here. And Emily Michelle. It looks as if Emily Michelle is coming down with a cold."

"I'm glad you're not alone," I said. "If someone called me while I was home alone, I'd
totally freak."

"I might, too," Kristy admitted.

What we didn't know then was that Mary
Anne *was* home alone.

And she was about to have a very unpleas-
ant visit.

Claudia called Mary Anne the moment she
hung up after talking with me.

When Mary Anne answered the phone, her
voice was somber.

"He called you, too?" asked Claudia.

"No. But I found another note today. It was
in my locker after school. And it doesn't make
any sense either. Listen: 'Why Do You Do the
Things You Do?' What things? What is it I'm
doing? Why doesn't Logan just tell me? If it
is Logan, I mean."

"Oh. The notes that Logan is sending you.
I thought it was something, ah, worse."

"Worse? What could be worse than your
boyfriend sending you weird notes? And you
know what? I think he's starting to act weird,
too. I mean, if he has a problem with what
I'm doing . . ." Mary Anne stopped. "Of
course, it just *looks* like his handwriting. I
mean, it probably isn't Logan. It's probably a
bad joke. An *extremely* bad joke."

114

"Mary Anne?" Claudia said gently. "Uh, Stacey and I have had more phone calls. We wanted to warn you. Stacey is calling Kristy. And the guy talked again."

Mary Anne's voice changed. "The anonymous phone caller? He talked? What did he say?"

"The same thing he said before: 'You're next.' "

Mary Anne said, "That's it. I'm not answering the phone anymore tonight. Not till Dad and Sharon come home."

Mary Anne told me later that after we hung up the phone, she looked at her watch. Her father and stepmother weren't due home for another hour. The house suddenly seemed very quiet.

In spite of herself, Mary Anne was drawn to the window. She stood to one side of it, pushed the edge of the curtain aside and peered out.

Nobody was out there. All was quiet and still. With a sigh of relief, Mary Anne turned around. She decided to go down to the kitchen and make some hot chocolate — and to check on the doors to make sure they were locked.

A few minutes later she was sitting at the kitchen table drinking hot chocolate when the cat door flipped open and Tigger slid through.

"Tigger," said Mary Anne. "It's cold outside! Aren't you freezing?"

Tigger wove himself in and out among the table legs, purring a giant purr.

"How about some warm milk?" Mary Anne suggested.

Her kitten purred even louder.

Mary Anne tilted the last bit of milk from the saucepan on the stove into a saucer. She put the saucer down for Tigger.

That was when she saw it.

Something white was attached to Tigger's collar. It had been taped to the tag with his name and address and phone number on it.

Surprised, Mary Anne picked Tigger up. He meowed protestingly and struggled to get back to his milk. She unfastened the piece of paper and put him back down.

It was a tightly folded square, like the notes kids pass at school. She unfolded it.

And gave a little scream.

It was a note, written with letters cut from the newspaper.

It said, "YOU'RE NEXT."

That freaked us all out. But it was, as Kristy pointed out, "hard evidence." She convinced Mary Anne to put the note in an envelope, "in case there were any fingerprints left," and to bring it to the BSC meeting the next day.

I was thinking about the note as I walked to Claudia's that Friday afternoon. I was also thinking about the crank calls, and yes, Shadow Lake.

It was late afternoon, one of those gloomy, shadowy, cold days that are completely depressing unless you're thinking, as I was, Hmmm, looks like it might snow.

I peered up at the sky. I stepped off the curb.

The car came out of nowhere.

I turned. It was heading toward me, picking up speed as it approached. It was a huge car, shiny and red and powerful-looking. The motor sounded like the roar of the subway, bearing down on me.

I froze.

I put my hands out as if that would stop the car, as if that would keep it from running right over me, from killing me.

This is it, I thought. I'm going to die.

I screamed and closed my eyes, and waited for the car to hit me. I had time to wonder if it would hurt.

The driver must have braked at the last minute. I heard the screech of tires as it swerved, and I opened my eyes as it hurtled past, inches away. I felt the wind brush my hands as the car sped by me.

I turned to watch it go. It careened crazily down the street and around the corner with another scream of tires.

I realized that I was standing in the street with my hands raised. I lowered them.

I hadn't been able to see the license plate number, although I'd seen that it was a Connecticut plate. But I'd recognized the Mercedes symbol on the hood. And I'd also recognized the blue hexagonal sticker on the rear bumper.

Whoever had almost run over me was a lousy driver in a very good car. And he — or she — was also a member of the Stoneybrook Business Bureau.

I don't remember the rest of the walk to the BSC meeting, or what I thought about, except one thing: I could hardly wait to get out of Stoneybrook. Things here were way, *way* out of control.

CHAPTER 11

Claudia

Friday

Friday

Stacey looked all shuck up when she got too the BSC meeting. She said it was proboly an acident. Abbey and Kristy didnt think so. They said it was part of the mystery.

I thought we should call the polise before sombody got killed or somthing.

Claudia

T he meeting was as much about the mystery as about baby-sitting, especially after Stacey came crashing through my bedroom door looking as if she'd seen a ghost.

When she told us what had happened, we were all freaked. I gave Stacey a glass of water and Mary Anne made her sit in a chair.

"It was an accident," Stacey said over and over.

"Even if it was an accident," I said, "you should report it to the police. That person could have killed you!"

Abby said, "And maybe it wasn't an accident."

Stacey managed a faint smile. "Well, it *wasn't*, technically. I mean, whoever it was swerved at the last minute and missed me. So I don't think the police could do anything, anyway."

"Could it be the man with the blue tattoo?" said Jessi suddenly.

Stacey's eyes widened. "You don't really think he's come back, do you?"

"Maybe," Kristy said. "I still think it's possible that this is *all* connected to those robbers we saw running out of Mr. Seger's house. I think we should include it in the mystery notebook."

120

"Right," I said. "Now. Who do we know who owns a red Mercedes?"

Silence fell. Then Mary Anne said, "That's easy — no one."

"Mr. Seger?" Mal wondered.

"Old blue Volvo," said Abby. "But well maintained."

Stacey said, "The blue sticker on the Mercedes was the same as the blue Business Bureau sticker on Mr. Seger's car, though."

Logan and Shannon had come to the meeting, because with four BSC members out of town, we would probably need their help this weekend. Logan, who was sitting next to Mary Anne, said, "We can keep an eye out for the red Mercedes this weekend." He nudged Mary Anne. "Can't we?"

Mary Anne asked, "Did you put the *anonymous note* I got with the other mystery clues, Mal?" She gave Logan a long, hard look.

Was it my imagination, or did Logan suddenly look uncomfortable?

Mal said, "I did."

"We'll all keep an eye on things," Shannon promised. "I'll even take Astrid for some nice long walks this weekend, and we'll check out Mr. Seger's house."

Then the phone rang, and club business occupied our attention for the next twenty minutes. By the time the phone stopped ringing, both Logan and Shannon had sitting jobs over the weekend.

When the phone was silent, Kristy said, "Speaking of snow . . ."

"It will snow," Abby said firmly. She held up her arms in a goal sign. "Ski Shadow Lake!"

I didn't say anything. It was weird to listen to Abby bragging about her skiing.

Stacey asked, very casually, "So, Kristy, how's Sam doing?"

"Cross as two sticks," said Kristy promptly. "He's the one who did the breaking up, but I don't think that makes him feel any better. Especially since she won't speak to him right now."

I knew Stacey was worried about Sam not just because he was recovering from a breakup, but because she was afraid he might rebound in her direction. At least, I thought, she didn't have to worry about Robert being a jealous jerk. She'd told him about Sam, and that Sam was going to be along on the trip, and Robert had just grinned and said, "Lucky Sam."

"Well, speaking of detective work, I'm going to take Becca along to Mal's house for our sitting job tomorrow," Jessi told us. "And I thought maybe we could go shopping, and sort of keep an eye out for the man with the blue tattoo. Maybe if Becca sees him while we're in a store or something, he won't seem so sinister. And I thought we could make it into a sort of game. You know, playing detective."

"You go have fun," said Mal stiffly to Jessi. "I'll stay at home with whoever doesn't feel like shopping, and work on the mystery notebook."

Kristy said, "Well, Watson came bounding up the stairs this morning and practically turned blue in the face. So I want you guys to promise that on this trip, you'll help me keep him from doing too much."

We promised we would.

Kristy looked at her watch. "This meeting of the BSC is officially adjourned."

"Allll right!" I cried. "Shadow Lake, here we come."

CHAPTER 12

Abby

Friday
Okay, the trip up to
Shadow Lake wasn't a
trip, it was an expedition.
I mean, we had eleven
people, including me.
Emily Michelle's cold
was worse, so Nannie
decided to stay home
with her. That meant
that Shannon (the puppy)
stayed home with
Nannie, too.
Still, there we were,
packed into the cars,
pulling out of the
driveway, waving good-
bye to Nannie, and
heading off for a
wonderful vacation.
That's sort of how
horror movies always
start, isn't it? Nice
and ordinary and
peaceful.
Ha.

"My skis," Kristy said with a gasp. "Did you put my skis in?"

"They're in the van," said Charlie, "with all of ours."

Stacey said, "You're sure I can rent skis when I get there?"

"Sure you can," Kristy told her as Charlie reached out for my skis.

"Hey, be careful with those," I warned him. I looked at Claudia, who was standing next to a large duffel bag. "Did he treat your skis like that?" I said. I was kidding, of course.

Charlie grinned. Claudia frowned. "No," she said.

"Hey, are you playing favorites? Or what?" I asked Charlie.

"The binding is broken on one of my skis," said Claudia. "I have to rent them."

"See, Stace? You can rent skis just like Claudia."

"Not if it doesn't snow," Kristy put in. Suddenly she leaped forward. "I'll take that," she said to Watson, and jerked a suitcase out of his hand so quickly he almost lost his balance. "Where do you want it?"

Watson looked surprised. "Uh, thanks, Kristy. It goes in the luggage rack on top of the station wagon."

Abby

Mr. Brewer was driving a van. Mrs. Brewer was driving a station wagon. If anybody had been hovering overhead in a helicopter, we would have looked like a bunch of ants on an anthill, running back and forth from the house to the cars, and from car to car, trying to pack everything in.

But at last all the gear was tied on, tucked in, stowed away, and accounted for. That left only the people.

Kristy said, "Why don't we divide up into two groups of two baby-sitters? We can keep an eye on Karen, David Michael, and Andrew."

"Fine by me," I said. "I think I'll go in the van. Keep an eye on the skis, too."

Claudia said, "Then I'll go in the station wagon."

Kristy looked faintly surprised, and I myself was a little taken aback at how grim Claudia sounded. Maybe she hadn't counted on baby-sitting on this trip. If she'd asked me, I could have told her that with Kristy around, we'd be organized into doing *something*.

Karen announced, "I am riding in the van. It has taller seats. You can look down into the cars you pass and see what is in them."

"It'll be dark, Karen," said David Michael. "It already is."

"Well, if the cars we pass have ghosts in

them, we will be able to see those in the dark," Karen began, her blue eyes growing huge behind her glasses. Karen has what some call a "vivid imagination." Sometimes I think she's plugged into Mars. I mean, I've never met a kid like her.

"Ghosts?" David Michael's eyes grew huge, too.

"We're not going to pass *any* cars full of ghosts," I said. "They only travel on Halloween. That's a ghost rule."

David Michael nodded seriously. But he said, "I think I'll ride in the station wagon."

Watson scooped Andrew up. "Why don't you ride in the van with us, Andrew?"

"Okay," said Andrew, and yawned. I could tell he'd be asleep in no time.

Charlie said, "The van for me."

Stacey looked from the car to the van. Then she looked at Sam, who was climbing into the station wagon, talking to David Michael. "I'll go in the van," she announced.

"Okay," said Kristy. She stopped. "Claud. Is something wrong?"

Claudia was glaring after Stacey. She said (with complete and obvious insincerity), "No."

I suddenly realized that Claudia and Stacey might want to ride in the same car together, because they were best friends. "Hey, you can go with Stacey," I said to Claudia. "No problem. Because I can — "

"I'm not a child," snapped Claudia. "Don't humor me!" She walked to the car with her nose in the air and got in.

I shrugged. I climbed in the van, and Kristy climbed in, too.

Mr. Brewer said, "Now, does anybody need to go to the bathroom?"

No one did.

We pulled out.

By unspoken agreement, we didn't mention the mystery we were leaving behind. I think we felt a guilty relief that we were out of it, at least for a long weekend. Andrew nodded off almost immediately. Karen, who'd claimed the seat in the front of the van next to Mr. Brewer, became his "chief navigator." She spent a lot of time pointing out signs and trying to figure out the mileage from the map by the light of a little reading lamp mounted on the dashboard. She also read us a great many interesting facts from the *Atlas of the United States* that Mr. Brewer kept under the passenger seat, including all the discounts we could get with the coupons at the back.

"But we're not stopping at a motel on the way, Karen," her father kept saying.

"I know," Karen would counter. "But if we did, listen to this!"

When we made a gas and bathroom stop, Andrew didn't even wake up. Kristy and I stayed in the van with him while everyone else piled out. Stacey returned to the van with a container of juice. "Claud needed french fries," she reported. "But I wasn't hungry."

Kristy frowned and said, "I hope Watson remembers to avoid fried foods. They're not good for his heart."

"Your mom's with him," Stacey pointed out. "I'm sure she'll remind him if he forgets."

"Oh. That's right." Kristy relaxed. Slightly.

"Chill, Agatha Kristy," I said. "We're on vacation here."

"Yeah." She paused. "I have to say I'm kind of relieved to be leaving Stoneybrook. It was beginning to shred my last nerve."

Stacey sighed. "Me, too. I just hope everyone else is okay. If someone's stalking the members of the BSC, for whatever crazy reason, it could get pretty hairy."

"We'll solve it soon," I said, sounding much more certain than I felt. I mean, solving mysteries is for Claudia's Nancy Drew books, right? It doesn't really happen all that often — not even to us.

Right?

Abby

Everyone piled into the station wagon and the van again, and then we were off. As we neared Shadow Lake, I was relieved to see snow on the ground. At least there was some snow for skiing, even if it was old.

Then Karen shrieked, "Shadow Lake! Sixteen miles!" We turned off the main road. We drove through a little town and then headed more or less uphill on a winding two-lane road.

And then we turned off that road and bumped down an even smaller road. A few minutes later, a big house with a porch that wrapped all the way around it came into view.

"That's a cabin?" I asked. I should have known that a "cabin" that could hold all the Brewer-Thomases and friends (including every member of the BSC) had to be huge. We walked into a big room with a fireplace, which was the kitchen, dining area, and living room all in one. Doors to the right and left of the living room led to two dormitory-style bedrooms, each with six bunkbeds in it. One room was for the girls and one was for the boys. Bathrooms were at the front end of each of the dorm rooms. Two small bedrooms and a bathroom were also at the far end of the living room.

The cabin was big, but pretty basic. There

were braided rag rugs on the worn wood floors throughout the cabin. In both dorm rooms were tables made of dark wood, and white bureaus. Patchwork quilts were folded neatly at the foot of every bed. Windows lined the outer walls of the dorms, looking out from beneath the eaves of the porch and into the woods.

It wasn't late, but suddenly, I found myself yawning as widely as Andrew had been. I realized I wasn't the only one. Karen's eyes were drooping behind her glasses, and David Michael was rubbing his eyes with his fists.

We might have stayed up, anyway. But Watson, entering the cabin with a suitcase (which he put down before Kristy could swoop in and grab it), said, "Whew! That's it."

"I'm tired!" Kristy said, suddenly and firmly. "I think we should turn in, catch some Zs, try for an early start."

"But . . ." Charlie began.

Kristy gave him a fierce look. I realized that Kristy was worried about Watson's overdoing it.

Fine by me. "I'm tired, too," I announced. I stretched and yawned.

Stacey and Claudia caught on, too. "Early to bed, early to rise and ski," said Stacey cheerfully.

Abby

Claudia said to Karen, "Lovely Ladies need their beauty sleep."

Karen nodded.

Charlie shrugged. "Okay."

We sorted out our luggage and claimed our bunks (Karen went for a top bunk, but the rest of us stayed low).

I was shocked at how dark it was when the lights went out. No houses nearby to give off light. No street lamps. No traffic signals.

No noise, either. Silence. Silence and darkness.

Good thing we left that mystery back in Stoneybrook, I thought sleepily. Or I might be pretty scared.

I yawned one more time and fell asleep.

First thing after breakfast the next morning, we decided to go exploring. Karen and David Michael wanted to go skating on Beaver Pond, a small pond near Shadow Lake that freezes over in the winter. Shadow Lake is so big and so deep in some places that it hardly ever freezes enough to be safe for ice-skating. Mrs. Brewer had decided to go with them. Mr. Brewer was taking Andrew to the bunny slope for some skiing, even though, as Kristy put it, the snow was so old it would probably wrinkle under your feet.

I could tell Kristy was disgusted with the lack of new snowfall, and I shared her feelings. (It wasn't cold enough to make snow yet.) I could live with old snow, if I had to, but I was willing to hold out a little while longer for some of the new stuff.

Charlie had found an old pair of snowshoes he wanted to try out. He and Sam spent most of breakfast arguing over them, until Watson pointed out that they could rent another pair at the lodge.

We all walked to the lodge together. I noticed that Sam had fallen into step with Stacey. "Ravishing here, isn't it?" Sam said to Stacey. Then for some reason, they both started laughing.

"Oh, brother," I heard Kristy mutter.

We split up when we reached the lodge. Kristy stood for a moment, watching Watson walk toward the ski rentals, hand in hand with Andrew. Watson was carrying his own skis, but Andrew didn't own any yet. He'd only been skiing once before.

Even though it was early on a Saturday morning, the lodge was jumping. We went to the information desk to see if they had any maps for hiking trails around Shadow Lake.

"Snowshoeing?" the woman behind the information desk asked. She was wearing a royal blue shirt with the words *Shadow Lake Lodge Staff* embroidered on the pocket in white.

"No, walking," Kristy replied.

"Ah. Well, you'll need to stay on pretty packed trails, then," the woman said. She rummaged around in a drawer and pulled out a map. She marked several trails with a pen. "These are good and packed. They're nice, not-too-long hikes."

"That one takes you to a waterfall," said a voice behind us.

We turned and saw a college-age guy with dark brown eyes and short, neatly cut, dark brown hair. He was holding a pair of snow-shoes under one arm.

"Thanks," said Kristy.

"I'm Woodie Keenan," he said. "Have you been here long?"

"Just since last night," Claudia said.

"Most people come up here to ski," he commented.

"We'll be skiing," I said. "Probably this afternoon."

"Could I have some help here?" a voice asked crossly. We looked around to see a tall, thin man with a thin mouth and thinning brown hair standing near the entrance of the lodge. He wore a patch over one eye which, with his mean expression, made him look sinister.

"Of course, Mr. Federman." A young blond man with a *Shadow Lake Lodge Staff* shirt hurried over to him. "What can I do for you?"

Mr. Federman scowled harder and pointed to a large package on the floor. "When I asked for this to be delivered to my cabin, I meant my cabin — not the front porch of the lodge," he said.

"Nice guy," I remarked.

Woodie Keenan was frowning. But all he said was, "Yup. Well, see you later."

"The waterfall?" suggested Stacey.

"Yes," said Claudia. "Let's do it."

We were almost out the door when a short, red-haired woman burst inside. She collided with me, and we both fell backward. She dropped the bag she had slung over one shoulder.

I bent to pick it up, but she grabbed it before I could hand it to her.

"I've got it!" she said sharply.

"Sorry. I didn't mean to bump into you," I said.

"It's all right." The woman looked over her shoulder, then around at all of us. She hurried to the information desk without another word.

"My key. Is it here?" she said breathlessly.

"I don't know. What's your name, please?" asked the clerk.

"Kris Renn. Ms. Kris Renn. Kris with a 'K,' R-E-N-N." Kris Renn looked over her shoulder again.

"And you are from?" the clerk prompted, her pen poised above the registration forms.

"Uh, New England. Uh, Maine," said Kris Renn. "You know. Portland."

The clerk didn't seem to notice Ms. Renn's agitation. She filled in the form calmly, then pushed it across the desk for Ms. Renn to sign.

"You like to ski?" the clerk asked pleasantly.

Ms. Renn said, "It's very popular in the winter here, isn't it?"

"It certainly is," said the clerk. She gave Ms. Renn the key.

Ms. Renn snatched it up and looked wildly around. I saw her look past where we were standing. I thought she appeared startled. Or maybe — afraid?

I turned quickly, but all I saw was the back of a man, climbing into one of the lodge cars.

When I turned back around, Ms. Renn was hurrying out one of the side doors of the lodge.

"You know," I remarked, "for people who are on vacation, some of these guys are way too tense and weird, if you ask me."

"Hey, it's not our problem," said Claudia. "We're here to have fun, remember?" Her voice had an edge to it.

"True," I said. I lowered my dark glasses. "Let's hit the trails."

CHAPTER 13

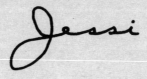

Jessi

Saturday

We have solved
The Case of the
Blue Tattoo. Or
at least, we have
solved part of it.
Kids are afraid
of the strangest
things. I mean,
where did my
little sister learn
to be afraid of
tattoos? Has she
ever actually met
anyone with a
tattoo? Hmmm.

Insulation equals isolation. At least, that seemed to be Mal's new philosophy of life, as I discovered when I reached the Pikes' house on Saturday morning. I could hear hammering and other construction (and presumably insulation) related sounds coming from the attic when I arrived. I was greeted in triplicate: the triplets, Adam, Byron, and Jordan, met me at the door.

"Hi, guys," I said. "Anybody home?"

It was a weak joke, but they thought it was funny. After much eye rolling and snorting and elbowing of one another, they let me in.

"Mal's in her room," said Adam. "She told us to keep an eye on things until you showed up."

I didn't like the sound of that. It's not that I think the triplets, who are ten, aren't capable of keeping an eye on the younger Pikes, namely, Vanessa (nine), Nicky (eight), Margo (seven), and Claire (five) in their own home with their parents on hand.

But "keeping an eye on" isn't the same as baby-sitting. Mal was not doing her job.

"So where is everybody? Besides Mal, I mean?" I asked casually.

"Watching TV," said Adam. He added, "We

were, too, but they wouldn't let us watch wrestling."

"Wrestling is on at this hour of the morning?" The thought didn't thrill me.

"Yeah! The Man of Molten Iron is taking on the Brickhouse Brothers," said Jordan enthusiastically.

Byron didn't say anything. He's the quietest of the triplets, and I suspected he wasn't as interested in wrestling as the other two.

"Well, why don't you go watch whatever it is the others are watching. I'll join you in a minute, and we'll think of something else to do." A good baby-sitter does not just park her charges in front of the television. I had no intention of doing that to the Pikes. But I wanted to have a word with Mal first.

Mal was sitting on her bed, the BSC notebook open in front of her and stacks of paper around her. She had stuck a pencil over one ear and a highlighter pen over the other.

That stopped me for a moment. "Wow," I said. "That looks like a bigger job than I thought."

"It is," said Mal. "Huge."

"The triplets tell me they've been keeping an eye on things. 'Things' is everybody watching television."

"That's nice," said Mal. She took her pencil,

wrote something on a piece of paper, put the pencil back, took the highlighter and high-lighted it, then put the paper on a stack.

"You want to help?" asked Mal in a not-very-encouraging voice.

"No, thanks," I said. "I have to baby-sit."

Mal knew what I was hinting at. But she didn't respond. She just made another note on another piece of paper.

I returned to the den full of Pikes. I was just in time. The triplets were playing catch with the remote control. The channels were flipping by at dizzying speed and the volume was set at full blast. Vanessa had set her hands on her hips and was stomping her foot. Margo and Nicky were leaping around the room trying to catch the remote in mid-pass. Claire's face was very, very red and I knew it was a matter of moments before she began to shriek. Or cry.

I made a grand jeté-save, grabbed the re-mote, and clicked off the television.

The silence was deafening. Everybody looked at me.

"Aw, what'd you do that for?" Jordan complained.

"What do you think?" I asked.

Jordan made a face.

There was a lot of pent-up energy in that room. Suddenly I had an inspiration. "How would you guys like to do some detective work?" I asked.

"You mean *play* detective?" Nicky asked.

"No, real detective work — if we can invite Becca over."

"I'll call her," said Vanessa instantly. She and my little sister Becca are good friends.

While we waited for Becca to arrive, I filled everybody in on her sighting of the man with the blue tattoo. "Becca's a little freaked out by the tattoo," I said. "And my friends and I think he might be a man we helped catch and send to jail for being a counterfeiter."

"Neatsy," said Claire. She wrinkled her brow. "What's a count and fitter?"

"Counterfeiter," I corrected her. "That's a person who makes fake money and then tries to use it like real money."

"Like Monopoly?" asked Claire.

"Sort of," I said. "But you can tell that Monopoly money isn't real. The only thing it will buy you is Monopoly property. The man with the blue tattoo made fake money that looked real and then spent it. Only it wasn't real, so the people who took it were cheated."

"Oh," said Claire. I wasn't sure she understood, but she seemed caught up in the idea of being a detective just the same.

Soon Becca arrived. We told her about our

plan to solve the Mystery of the Man With the Blue Tattoo. She didn't exactly look thrilled, but, like Claire, she went along with the enthusiastic crowd.

"Okay, triplets, you're in charge of seeing that everyone is bundled up warmly enough. It's pretty chilly outside. I'm going to get Mal and we'll let your parents know where we are going."

Mal hadn't moved from her spot on the bed.

"Mallory Pike," I said. "You are supposed to be helping me baby-sit. I know you're mad because you didn't get to go to Shadow Lake. But it's not fair to sulk in your room and leave me to do all the work."

Mallory looked startled. "Oh!" she exclaimed. Then her cheeks reddened. "Was that what I was doing? I guess it was. I'm sorry."

"Good," I said. "We're going on a Blue Tattoo Manhunt, so come on."

Mal grinned sheepishly. "Okay," she said.

And that was that.

A few minutes later, we were headed out the door. Mr. and Mrs. Pike, both of whom were wearing masks like the ones Abby sometimes wears on bad allergy days, were wrestling big pink rolls of insulation around the attic. They seemed almost relieved when we said we were going out. Mr. Pike gave us money, in case we wanted to get a pizza for lunch.

"The bright side of insulation, I guess," Mal remarked, putting the money in her pocket.

Traveling with a large group of kids, especially the Pike kids, with triplets among them, is a guarantee that you will not be anonymous. (I was glad we weren't trying to stake out Mr. Seger's house!) And traveling with a large group of kids who are trying to be detectives is pretty daunting, both for the baby-sitters and for the unwary passersby.

"Where was this tattoo?" I asked Becca.

"On his face," she said in a small voice. She squinted her eyes tightly shut for a moment.

"Did it cover his whole face?" asked Vanessa, looking worried.

"Was it a monster? Something good?" asked Jordan.

"Oh, ick, you're sick," said Vanessa.

"It wasn't a monster," said Becca. "I don't remember. It was just blue, that's all."

· "We'll find him," said Nicky.

That meant that every male passerby was subject to the full force of eight pairs of eyes, staring penetratingly at his face. And of course, Mal and I looked, too. We just tried to be more discreet about it.

One man smoothed his hair back nervously.

Another man with bushy eyebrows frowned menacingly. Several men pretended not to notice at all.

Nicky was staring so hard that he walked into a fence. Fortunately, he wasn't hurt.

"Too bad it wasn't wet paint," said Adam. "That would've been cool."

Mal and I exchanged a glance while the triplets and Nicky snickered.

When we reached downtown Stoneybrook, we divided the group into partners. When we passed the post office, Vanessa dragged us over to it so we could look at the wanted posters. But the post office was closed.

"I don't think his poster would have been up in the post office, Vanessa," I said. "Wanted posters are for people who haven't been caught yet. And we don't even know if this is the same guy."

"But he could be in there," she insisted. "What if he *is* the same guy, and he escaped from jail, and he's come back to Stoneybrook to get revenge?"

Becca, who was Vanessa's partner, suddenly looked very worried.

I felt a pang of fear. This was too close to what we thought the burglars were doing — stalking the BSC.

Quickly I said, "Well, it's not the same guy."

145

Jessi

Vanessa opened her mouth to argue but then Jordan said, "I think we should look in the hardware store."

"The toy store," said Margo.

"Toys," echoed Claire.

"Hardware," said Vanessa. "Hammers and nails and insulation and pails."

Mal whispered, "See? It's catching. Now Vanessa is making *rhymes* about insulation."

We split up to continue our search. Not surprisingly, no one saw a man with a blue tattoo in either the hardware store or the toy store, although the kids saw many, many other interesting things.

Then Margo suggested we look for the tattooed man at the ice-cream shop.

"No," I said firmly.

I looked at Mal. She patted her pocket. "We *could* look for him at the pizza parlor," she said. "That is, if anybody wants to eat pizza for lunch."

The vote was loudly and unanimously in favor of continuing our search there.

We chose the good old Pizza Express. Of course, the Pikes and Becca were already deep into the argument about what kind of pizza we were going to order before we even reached the counter.

We stopped.

Becca tugged on my arm so hard it almost came out of its socket.

"Ow. What is it, Becca? What's wrong?"

She pointed. "It's him!" she whispered. "It's the man with the blue tattoo!"

For the second time that day, all the Pikes were silent.

We stared at the man behind the counter — not the one waiting to take our order, but the one making salad.

"Nothing like a good fresh salad, is there, Pete?" he said to someone else in the kitchen who we couldn't see.

The someone said something in reply, and the man with the blue tattoo said, "The secret is, you make it fresh from scratch every day."

"May I help you?" asked the guy who was taking orders.

We all looked at him. Finally Mal regained her senses, or at least some of them. "Yes," she said. "We'd like a blue . . . a pizza."

"Blue pizza we don't have. You want a few more minutes?"

"Yes," said Mal.

We retreated. "It's him," I said. "But is it *him*? You know, the counterfeiter?"

"Nope," said Mal. "I remember that description from the notebook. The counterfeiter's blue tattoo was on his earlobe. This tattoo is on the guy's cheek."

I was suddenly enormously relieved.

We made our pizza decision and went back to the counter. It was only after we placed our order that I realized that Becca had melted to the back of the group. She was still keeping a close eye on the salad-making tattooed man.

"Becca," I said softly. "It's okay. See? It's just a tattoo. Like . . . like permanent makeup. Or face-painting."

"I don't like it," said Becca firmly.

She kept watching him while she ate her pizza. And she looked back over her shoulder half a dozen times as we walked home.

"He's not going to hurt you," I reassured her. "He's just an ordinary guy, you know. With a tattoo. Lots of people have tattoos."

"Yes," said Becca.

There was only one thing to do.

Back at the Pikes', I whispered in Mal's ear.

· "I'll ask Mom," said Mal. "Great idea. I'll be right back."

She returned in a few minutes with a shoe-box full of old makeup.

"I'm *not* wearing makeup," said Nicky immediately.

"You mean you don't want a tattoo?" asked Mallory.

That got his interest. It got everyone's — except, at first, Becca's. She still hung back. She watched as we drew designs on the Pikes' arms and cheeks with eyebrow pencil and eyeliner, then filled them in with eyeshadow and lipstick.

Then suddenly, she asked, "Could I have a butterfly tattoo?"

"Sure," I said casually.

We played "tattoo" most of the afternoon. I was getting ready to leave when I heard Vanessa say, "Oh, oh, oh, let it snow, snow, snow."

I stepped outside and looked up at the sky. Sure enough, big, fat, white flakes were spiraling down.

I hoped they were doing the same at Shadow Lake.

Kristy

Saturday

The snow fell. And fell. And fell.
At the lodge, they said it wasn't just
going to be a snowstorm, but a blizzard.
The moment the snow started to fall,
I was ski-slope bound, dragging
Abby and Stacey and Claudia with me.
I wasn't about to let a little thing like
a blizzard stop me.

As it turned out, the blizzard wasn't
the problem. We had something much,
much worse to worry about. . . .

Kristy

"Isn't it beautiful?" said Claudia, holding out her mittened hand to catch the snowflakes that were falling, faster and faster, from the gray sky.

"Beautiful," I said. "Come on." I took off down the trails we'd been wandering around all morning and hustled everybody back to our cabin, so we could eat a quick lunch and grab Abby's and my skis. Claudia barely had time to slip a Ring Ding into her jacket pocket for nourishment out on the slopes before we were standing in line at the ski rental desk.

The guy behind the desk was cute. His blue eyes matched his shirt. I noticed this, but I wasn't interested.

Stacey and Claudia noticed it, too. But I didn't let them hang around. "Here," I said impatiently to Stacey. "You buckle your ski boot like this."

Stacey and the staff guy looked startled, but at least she had her boots on.

As I straightened up, Abby put her elbow into my side. This is a bad habit she really needs to break. Where does she learn these things?

I was about to point this out to her when she said, "Look!"

I looked. In fact, we all looked.

I'd dropped my ski gear bag at the end of the bench, along with Abby's, plus Stacey's backpack which she'd brought along (I suspected she had stuck her purse in there). The guy with the eye patch was bending over them.

"I could kill them," he said as clearly as if no one at all was standing around listening. "They'd deserve it. No jury in the world would convict me. . . ."

He looked up. His face was twisted and his eye blazed.

We shrank back.

"Mr. Federman?" said the staff guy uncertainly.

Mr. Federman spun around and stomped away.

"Wow," breathed Stacey. "I hope I don't run into him out on the slopes."

I was staring after Mr. Federman. "Let's check our stuff. The way he looked, I want to make sure he didn't stick a bomb in there or something."

"Why do you think he was so angry? Was he angry at us?" Claudia asked.

"Why would he be? We've never seen him before, until this morning," Abby answered practically.

We got our gear (it was bomb-free) and

stowed it in the lockers. Then we headed out to the lifts.

I kept seeing Mr. Federman's face and the way he had looked at us. Had we done something to offend him? Did we know him from somewhere else? It was an odd, unsettling incident. But when I saw all that excellent new powder covering the slopes, I forgot about Mr. Federman.

We decided to split up. I wanted to head for a beginner trail, to warm up. Stacey wanted to practice on the little slope where the lessons for beginners were given (it was hardly more than a bump).

"It's a good idea to start out slow," said Abby, looking thoughtfully up the mountain. "I'm not familiar with these slopes. I mean, sure a green circle means beginner and a slope marked with a blue square means intermediate and all. But I think I'd better check out what they mean by intermediate before I do the expert runs. . . . Claudia, you want to go with me?"

"Gee, thanks. You think I could handle a big intermediate slope?" said Claudia in a sarcastic tone of voice.

Stacey and I exchanged a surprised glance. Why was Claudia being so prickly? And so rude to Abby? I mean, sure Abby is a little bossy, a little overwhelming, but she didn't mean anything by it.

Abby, who hasn't known Claudia all that long, just laughed. "Sure," she said.

"I'm just surprised you're not starting out on the black diamond trails," Claudia said.

Stacey said quickly, "Even I know those are for the super experts, Claudia. No one does those unless they're practically in the Olympics."

"Well. . . ." Abby said, and grinned modestly. "Come on, Stacey. Once you're warmed up, you're going to be moguling all over this mountain."

"Moguling? You mean hitting bumps and flying into the air?"

"And landing without falling," agreed Abby.

"Let's meet back here in about an hour for a hot-chocolate break," I suggested.

Everyone agreed, and we went our separate ways.

Abby was right. A couple of slides down the practice slope and Stacey was ready for the beginners' runs. It all came back to her, just like riding a bike.

Stacey shivered. "It's getting colder."

"Don't say that!" I exclaimed. "You know if it gets too cold it won't snow anymore."

154

Stacey laughed. "I guess when I start moving, I'll warm up."

"I have some extra glove liners and socks in my gear bag. You can borrow some when we take our hot chocolate break," I said.

"Great," said Stacey. "See you then."

"See ya," I replied, and headed toward a lift in the opposite direction.

Stacey got in line for the nearest beginner trail. There were only a couple of people ahead of her.

She was cool about skiing, now, but she'd forgotten how to get in the lift chair. Hesitating, she missed the first chair and then the second before she hit the timing right. She was embarrassed, even though the lift operator at the bottom was cool about it, and no one was behind her in line.

Once she was in the lift, she forgot her embarrassment. She looked around, marveling at how snow made everything look different. Mysterious. Special.

At first she didn't even notice that the lift had stopped.

Then she thought that it had just stopped for a moment because someone was having trouble getting off, just as she had had trouble getting on.

Then she realized that she was the only one

on the lift. And that the snow was blowing harder, and the lift chair was swinging back and forth.

And it was getting even colder.

"Hey!" she said. "Hey! Hello!"

No one answered. A tiny figure skied by below and disappeared down the slope. Stacey peered up ahead. She couldn't see anyone in the lift booth. It was barely visible in the swirling snow.

"Hello!" she shouted. "Hello?"

Still no answer.

This is silly, thought Stacey. She waited. And waited.

And felt colder and colder.

"Hello!" she called. And then, beginning to panic, "Help! Help!"

She was stuck on the ski lift.

It was the sudden blast of snow that sidetracked me, sending me spinning almost out of control. The snow wasn't anywhere near up to blizzard speed yet, I'd decided. In fact, it was falling nice and evenly. No visibility problems.

Excellent powder.

After those beginner slopes I'd tried an intermediate. I checked my watch and decided that if the line wasn't too long, I had time for one more intermediate run. I found a new one, off to one side, where almost no one was skiing, probably because it was a long clomp in your skis to the bottom of the lift.

I was halfway down the slope when the snow turned into a blinding blizzard, a blast that hit me in the face so hard I lost my balance. I swerved. I brought the tips of my skis together in a snowplow to slow myself down.

Then I heard a roar. An avalanche! I thought confusedly, although of course, this wasn't possible on the slope where I was skiing.

I tried to see where I was going. For a moment, I thought I saw something looming up ahead of me. Then I hit a mogul, shot up into the air, and landed hard on my back. I felt my skis turn with a sickening wrench under me.

"Are you having fun yet?" Abby asked cheerfully, catching up to Claudia and jumping into the lift chair with her on the way up to the expert slopes.

"Do you always follow people around?" answered Claudia. "Or did you just come to give me a ski lesson of my own?"

That got through to Abby. She turned to face Claudia. "What are you talking about?"

"I'm surprised you didn't drag Stacey up here. I mean, since you're such a great skier and all. Couldn't you turn her into an expert in one easy lesson?"

"Whoa," said Abby, genuinely surprised.

Claudia looked a little ashamed of herself. But she just shrugged.

They jumped off the ski lift. Claudia took off without waiting for Abby, or even looking at her.

Abby stood back. For some reason, Claudia was making it even colder out on the mountain than it already was. Then Abby squinted against the glare of the snow. Claudia was veering off to the left.

Something clicked in Abby's brain. She whipped the trails map out of her pocket. Sure enough, there was a trail a short way down the mountain. A double black diamond trail.

Was Claudia actually going to try a double diamond run?

"Claudia!" Abby shouted.

Then she looked at the map again and her heart began to pound fast and furiously. The trail Claudia was heading for was marked DANGER: CLOSED FOR SEASON in big red letters.

"I don't know what happened," the woman said. "Somehow, this got down into the works and completely jammed everything up." She

158

held up the greasy, mangled remnant of what looked like a ski hat, a pink one with a white pom pom on top.

Stacey was shivering. "But — but — " she stammered.

"Someone is usually working up here, but it was between shifts. In fact, I was just coming on shift when you went up."

"How long was I up there?" Stacey asked.

The woman looked Stacey over. "Long enough, I'd say. . . . Joe, give Stacey a ride down to the lodge in the snowmobile, and all the hot chocolate she wants — on the house."

Zipping past skiers in the snowmobile would have cheered Stacey up, normally, especially since Joe, like most of the other staff members at Shadow Lake Lodge, was very cute. But she was too cold and numb to do more than watch mutely as the lodge came closer and closer. She staggered into the lodge, requested sugarless hot chocolate, and collapsed in a big, overstuffed chair practically in the fireplace, which is where I found her when I returned.

Stacey looked up from the cup of hot chocolate she was cradling in her hands.

"Kristy!" she cried. "What happened to you?"

At the same moment, I said, "Stacey? Are

you okay?" I shivered suddenly. Snow had worked its way underneath my skiing gear. I was wet and cold.

"Hot chocolate," said Stacey. "Get some and pull a chair up to the fire."

I obeyed. A little while later I was warming my hands around my mug and my feet at the fire and listening to Stacey say, "They think it was one of those freak accidents. But I was scared. I kept thinking, What if this lift chair just breaks off and I fall?" She shivered, this time not from cold.

"That's what they said about what happened to me, too," I said. "A snowblower came on when I was halfway down the trail. It was lucky I was the only one on that section of trail right then." I remembered the whiteness that had suddenly engulfed me, and speeding blindly toward what looked like a tree before hitting the mogul and getting buried in the snow. "The worst thing was, I heard something snap when I fell. I was sure it was my ankle."

"Oh, Kristy," said Stacey.

"Well, it wasn't, but I'd flattened this little tree. They don't know how the snowblower got turned on. Some of the ski staff came and helped me down the mountain." I made a face. "Everybody was staring at me. I felt like one of those stupid jerks who goes up on a hard slope and then has to be helped down."

I looked at my watch. "It's been nearly two hours," I said. "Abby and Claudia should be here."

Stacey met my eyes. "They weren't getting along so well, were they? You don't think one of them pushed the other down the mountain, do you?"

"Admit it, Abigail Stevenson," a familiar voice said, "the Ring Ding gave us the energy to get down the mountain."

"Yeah, well, I don't think it would have broken your fall," answered Abby dryly.

We looked up. Claudia and Abby were crossing the lodge toward us, their arms around each other like old friends, or as if each was helping the other to walk.

As it turned out, it was a little of both.

Stacey and I were stunned when we heard what had happened to Claudia.

"A closed black diamond trail!" I gasped. "Claudia, you could have been killed!"

"If it had all been open, she probably could have managed it, with a little luck," said Abby. "She's a pretty good skier. It was the closed, dangerous part that almost did her in."

"Yeah. Dangerous, as in part of the trail has collapsed and is now a ravine," said Claudia.

She looked suddenly somber. "If Abby hadn't grabbed me from behind, I don't know what would have happened. I don't think I could have stopped in time, although I was certainly trying."

"That's awful," Stacey cried. "Why wasn't the trail better marked?"

"Someone on the ski staff saw us and came to help," said Abby. "He found the first 'DANGER/CLOSED' sign half-buried in the snow about ten feet from the trail head."

Claudia said, "He said there's no way it could have landed there by accident. And that it was there this morning before they opened the trails, and at lunch when the ski patrol checked them again."

I put my hands to my head. "Three wipe-outs in one day. Abby, you are the only one who hasn't had bad luck."

Stacey said, "You think it was just bad luck?"

I stared down in my hot chocolate. No answers there. I finally said, "Bad luck. Or worse. If I didn't know better, I'd think our mystery had followed us up here."

When we were warm enough and dry enough, and couldn't drink another drop of hot chocolate, we made our weary way back to the cabin.

And found the door standing wide open.

"Don't go in," said Claudia urgently. "What if there's a — a maniac lurking?"

For a moment, I almost believed her. Then I said, "Claud, if anybody is there, I'll scream. You guys run for help."

Of course, no one was there. But the cabin was *freezing*.

"Mitch must have come to deliver wood and left the door open enough for the wind to catch it," I said, after we'd checked out the cabin and made sure that nothing was missing or had been disturbed.

Everyone else looked relieved. But I was still spooked. Mitch is the caretaker, and he is very neat and responsible. It wasn't like him to be so careless.

When Watson came home, he spooked me even further. "Firewood? Mitch? No, there's no reason for Mitch to be here. We have plenty of firewood." He turned around and began putting his coat on again.

"Watson," I said. "Where are you going?"

"To find Mitch. See what's going on."

"Wait! I'll go," I volunteered.

"That's nice of you, Kristy. But I don't think this is your job." Watson walked after him.

I hurried to the door. How could he go out again when he'd been out all day, skiing and

163

doing who knew what else. He must be exhausted. I had a sudden, horrible vision of him falling down in the snow on the way to the lodge, his hand to his chest, trying to breathe. . . .

"Watson, stop!" I shrieked. I leaped off the porch and down the path in two giant steps.

Watson turned, looking very surprised.

"Stop," I panted. "You have to stop doing this."

"Doing what?"

"This! Too much! The doctor told you not to exert yourself. He said you were supposed to take it easy. And all you do is . . . is . . ."

"Kristy," said Watson, putting his arm around me and pulling me into a hug. "Is that what this is all about — helping me with the luggage, jumping up to fetch things for me, always bringing me slippers and sweaters?"

I nodded.

"Oh, Kristy." Watson held me at arm's length. "I'm not doing too much. I had a check-up before we came here. Everything is going perfectly. In fact, I'm supposed to start exercising seriously on a regular basis. I'm even thinking of taking up jogging."

"The doctor said you could?" I asked.

"The doctor said I should. And there's a doctor on staff at the lodge. She lives here in

Shadow Lake. So even if something did go wrong, which I very much doubt, a doctor would be on hand."

I sighed. I felt a little silly. Watson was taking care of himself. I just hadn't trusted him.

You know what? I didn't want Watson disappearing the way my father had. I wanted Watson around for a long, long time. Like forever.

I gave Watson a quick hug. "Okay," I said. "I'm freezing."

"Go in the house," said Watson, giving me a quick hug back.

I dashed up the stairs. When I reached the top Watson said, "Kristy?"

I turned. Watson smiled at me. A family, fatherly smile. "Thanks," he said.

CHAPTER 15

Mary Anne

Saturday

Rodowsky-sitting is always interesting. But this time, it was a little too interesting. In fact, it was, well, criminally interesting.

Archie had watched his *Aladdin* video (which I think he's seen a hundred times — he knows all of the genie's lines, even though I don't think he understands more than half of them) and had gone to bed quietly. He was sound asleep now.

I sent Shea and Jackie to take their baths, told them I'd be upstairs to check on them (I didn't want Jackie to flood the bathroom accidentally) and promised them popcorn and hot chocolate when they were clean and in their pajamas.

Then I stood at the kitchen window and stared out at the Segers' house, thinking about Logan, who was at the football banquet. I thought about the new sweater I'd bought for our special date tomorrow night. I wondered if Logan had sent me those strange notes. And why.

If he had sent them, maybe he wasn't the Logan I thought I knew.

The idea made me feel very lonely and confused.

I was thinking so hard about Logan (and listening to the sounds of Jackie and Shea running bathwater) that the battered Ford Escort had pulled into the driveway and stopped before I noticed it. For a moment, I thought Mr.

Mary Anne

Seger had come home. Then I remembered that right after I'd arrived at the Rodowskys', I'd seen a woman go to the front door of his house and ring the bell, and that he'd left with her, in her car. His car was still in the driveway.

Some instinct made me turn away from the window. A moment later, I'd turned out the light and rushed back to the window.

It was the same kind of car that Kristy and Abby had described the burglars as driving.

I knew that with the light out, no one could see me standing at the window. But I still peered out cautiously. The streetlights gave off enough light for me to see pretty clearly.

Noah Seger got out of the passenger side of the car. From the other side, a very short person emerged.

Short. Just like the burglar Kristy and Abby had seen.

Noah and his friend looked around carefully. They even looked over at the Rodowskys', which made me shrink back.

But they didn't see me. Noah nodded and said something.

Then they went into the house. Except they didn't use the door. They pried open the window!

I didn't think. I just leaped for the phone and called the police.

"Sergeant Johnson, please," I said breathlessly. "It's *urgent*."

I told Sergeant Johnson what I'd seen.

"I'll be right over," he said. "Don't do anything. Stay where you are."

I wasn't about to argue. Besides, I was babysitting. That was my first responsibility.

I hung up the phone, checked on Jackie and Shea, who were now in their PJs and playing a computer game. I promised them popcorn and hot chocolate later. Then I went back to the kitchen and stared at the dark house across the way.

It was unnerving. Where were the police?

Almost without noticing what I did, I picked up the phone and called Logan. He answered. He'd just come home from the football banquet. He didn't sound all that happy to hear from me, I thought, but I couldn't worry about that now. I told him what I'd seen and he said he'd come right over, too.

Things became a little crazy after that. Oh, the police car didn't arrive with its light flashing and its siren blaring or anything like that. In fact, it glided up to the curb silently, like a shark. Sergeant Johnson, and his partner, Ser-

geant Tang, had just gotten out of their car
when another car pulled up.

Oh, my lord. It was Mr. Seger. Mr. Seger
got out of the car, saw the police car, and
sprinted for it. The car he'd been in drove
away.

The Rodowskys pulled into their driveway.

A bicycle came careening after them.

I threw open the front door. "Logan," I said.
"Mr. and Mrs. Rodowsky."

The Rodowskys hurried out of the car and
followed Logan up the walk. Sergeant Tang,
Sergeant Johnson, and Mr. Seger were right
behind them.

"Is something wrong?" asked Mrs. Rodowsky. "Are the boys all right?"

"They're fine," I said. "But I saw someone
breaking into the house next door."

Before I could say anything else, Sergeant
Johnson said, "I want everybody to stay here."

"Please," Mr. Seger began.

"It'll be all right, Mr. Seger," said Sergeant
Tang.

"Shea and Jackie are playing computer
games," I told the Rodowskys. "They're all
ready for bed. Archie is asleep. I called Logan
when I saw the burglars — after I called the
police — because, because . . ."

Mr. Rodowsky patted my shoulder. "I understand." He said to Mrs. Rodowsky, "I'll just go take a look at the boys."

The police officers had gone outside again. "The kitchen," I said, suddenly remembering. "We can see from the window over the sink."

We reached the kitchen window just as Sergeant Tang and Sergeant Johnson reached the side door of the house.

The door opened.

The two officers crouched down.

Someone leaned out, looked around, stepped back inside. Then he began to back out of the house.

It was Noah and his friend. And they were carrying a television set.

"Noah," gasped Mr. Seger, and in spite of what Sergeant Johnson and Sergeant Tang had told us, we found ourselves outside with Noah and the police in Mr. Seger's driveway.

Noah was saying, "Oh, no. I can't believe this. . . . I'm sorry. It's just a joke . . . a . . ."

"Burglary is no joke," said Sergeant Tang.

"It's my own house! How could I . . ."

Mr. Seger made some small, distressed sound and Noah's voice trailed off. Then Noah said, "You're right. I was taking the television to sell. We took some stuff once before, too,

James and me, when some kids saw us."

James didn't say anything. He just folded his arms and looked unhappy.

"I thought it was you, but I didn't know why," said Mr. Seger.

"I owe money," said Noah. "Lots of money. I don't know how I am going to pay it back."

"You could have asked me," said Mr. Seger. "I would have given it to you. We could have worked something out."

Noah hung his head. "I'm sorry," he said softly.

Sergeant Tang said, "I think if we go down to the station and have a little talk, we might be able to work something out."

"Am I going to go to jail?" asked Noah, looking very frightened and very young.

"We'll talk," said Sergeant Johnson.

As Mr. Seger and Noah and James walked to the patrol car with Sergeant Tang, I said, "Uh, Noah? Could I ask you a question?"

Noah turned to look over his shoulder. He seemed surprised to see me, as if he hadn't noticed me before. "What?"

"Have you and, uh, James, been bothering me and my friends? I mean, two of my friends saw you, and we're all members of a club together, the Baby-sitters Club, and some strange things have been happening to us, and I wondered . . ."

Noah said, "I wouldn't pick on a bunch of kids."

Kids. Well. Who did he think had helped catch him?

But I didn't say anything.

James asked, "Were you one of the kids I saw?"

"No," I asked. "It was two of my friends."

"Oh," said James, losing interest in me altogether.

"You've done a good job here," said Sergeant Johnson. "Once again, the Baby-sitters Club has helped solve a crime." He grinned. "Maybe you should change your name to the Crime Busters Club."

Logan and I smiled. Sergeant Johnson left. Mrs. Rodowsky went back in the house.

So the burglars hadn't been the ones who were haunting the BSC, I thought, as I watched the police car drive away. I slid my hand into Logan's, forgetting for a moment about the anonymous notes.

If Noah and James weren't the BSC stalkers, then who was?

CHAPTER 16

LOGAN

SUNDAY

IT HADN'T BEEN JUST ANOTHER SATURDAY NIGHT, THAT WAS FOR SURE. BETWEEN THE FOOTBALL BANQUET AND THE BURGLARY, I WAS BEAT. I WAS NOT LOOKING FORWARD TO THE SUNDAY MEETING OF THE BSC THAT HAD BEEN CALLED AT SHANNON'S HOUSE, — ABOUT WHICH I HAD BEEN INFORMED BY A PHONE CALL AT THE CRACK OF DAWN (IT SEEMED) FROM MARY ANNE. PLUS, I WASN'T SURE I WANTED TO SEE MARY ANNE AGAIN.

We met in the den at Shannon's house, which has a sliding glass door that looks out over the backyard. The view was of snow, lots of it, and a leaden gray sky. I could tell the sky held more snow. I just wondered where all that snow was going to go.

Mary Anne looked up quickly when I walked in, as if she were startled to see me, then looked away. I hurried past her and sat down by Mal, who was holding a big, black looseleaf notebook open on her lap.

"I've been telling everyone what happened last night," said Mary Anne, not quite meeting my eyes.

Jessi said, "Wow, I can hardly wait to baby-sit at night. That's when all the good stuff happens."

We laughed at that. Then Shannon said, "It sounds as if we've solved one mystery and found another that's even worse."

"Yeah. If those guys weren't stalking the BSC, who is doing it? And why?" I asked.

Mal held up the notebook. "We can go over the clues and see if that helps," she said.

She flipped through the book and I saw that she'd put page dividers in it and everything. Mallory had done an awesome organizing job.

We went over our notes and clues, but it

didn't add up to much. The only real clue was
the red Mercedes with the Connecticut plates
and the blue sticker that had tried to run Stacey down — if you didn't count the nasty note
that had been delivered to Mary Anne via Tigger. And we couldn't make much of that, since
it was letters cut from a newspaper and pasted
on plain paper.

Someone who didn't want his handwriting
to be recognized, I thought, and remembered,
with a little jolt, the strange, whacked-out
notes I'd been getting from Mary Anne in her
distinctive, loopy handwriting.

"DON'T YOU DARE," one had said. Don't
I dare what? "LIES AREN'T THE TRUTH,"
the next one had said. What had I ever lied
to Mary Anne about?

Why didn't she trust me anymore?

Why wouldn't she talk to me about it?

And now I was pretty sure she was avoiding
me.

Shannon said, "Well, if the blue sticker was
the one for last year's Business Bureau, why
isn't there one for this year? Why isn't there
an orange one, like the orange one Mr. Seger
has on his car?"

"Whoever it is, isn't a member anymore,"
said Mal.

"Right," said Shannon. "That's a definite possibility."

Jessi sat bolt upright. "So if we compare the two lists the Business Bureau secretary gave us, we can find out who was on the list last year who isn't on it this year."

The words were barely out of her mouth before Mal had flipped the mystery notebook open again and pulled out the lists.

We came up with three names.

One of the names was Karl Tate, the formerly rich real estate man who'd been caught by Dawn and the BSC in a dognapping scheme. He'd gone to jail.

That was why he wasn't a member of the bureau anymore.

"Did Karl Tate have a Mercedes?" I asked. "A red Mercedes?"

"Let me see," said Mal, flipping toward the front of the mystery notebook. "Wow. Look at this. It says that Mrs. Tate was driving a red Mercedes. Maybe it's her car. Or maybe it's his."

"Yeah, well, he can't drive it in jail," I pointed out.

"What if he isn't still in jail?" suggested Mary Anne softly.

"There's one way to find out," said Shannon, reaching for the phone and the phone book. A few minutes later she was talking to Sergeant Johnson.

When she hung up, she looked solemn. "He's been released," she said. "For good behavior."

"But even if he was out, how would he know that anyone in the BSC was involved in catching him . . ." Jessi's voice trailed off. Then she said, "The picture in the *Stoneybrook News*. The one Abby found by the photocopier at the library."

Shannon picked up the phone again.

"Who're you calling now?" I asked.

She held up a finger, then said, "Hello? Mrs. Tate? Is Mr. Tate there? . . . Do you know when he'll be back? . . . A few days? Do you know where I could reach him? . . . Oh, just a, ah, friend. . . . No, no message. Thank you."

She looked grimly around at us. "Mr. Tate is out of jail. He's also out of town, and has been for a few days, according to Mrs. Tate."

"He's the one!" said Mary Anne, putting her hands to her cheeks. "That's why nothing has happened! He's out of town. And that really is why it's only Claudia and Kristy and Stacey and I that all this stuff has been happening to."

178

"Because he saw your picture, with the article about how we helped to capture him, in the newspaper." Mal's face was suddenly pale, and the faint dusting of freckles on her face stood out. "We weren't in the photo, but you were. He's out of jail and he's out for revenge — against you."

"We have to call Kristy and the others at Shadow Lake and warn them!" Mary Anne cried. "He could already be there!"

For the third time, Shannon picked up the phone. She called information for Shadow Lake, and asked for the number for Watson Brewer. She gave that and the phone to Mary Anne.

"Stacey!" cried Mary Anne a few seconds later. "Is that you? Are you all right?"

She listened for a moment and said, "Oh, no. Stacey, can you hear me? . . . Okay. They caught the Seger burglar. . . . No, I'll tell you about it later. This is much, much more important. It wasn't him who was bothering you. It was Karl Tate. . . . Stacey? Can you hear me? . . . Karl Tate! He's out of jail and . . . Stacey? Stacey! STACEY!"

CHAPTER 17

Stacey

Sunday

Shadow Lake is primitive. This means that the phones in the cabins, even a big cabin like Watson's, are old-fashioned. It also means that the phones can go out at any time and leave you stranded, miles from help, alone in the middle of nowhere....

Stalked by a maniac.

"Hello?" I shouted into the phone. But Mary Anne's voice, coming over the wires from Shannon's den that Sunday, had stopped abruptly.

I gave the phone a thump. I still couldn't hear Mary Anne.

"Karl Tate," I muttered. Was that what I had heard? Why had Mary Anne hung up so suddenly? Then I realized that the phones were down. The blizzard had officially arrived.

I left the small bedroom where the phone was and entered the main room of the cabin, where everyone had just finished breakfast.

"That was Mary Anne," I announced. "But I couldn't understand or hear everything she was saying, and then the phone went dead."

"The phone lines must be down," said Watson, standing up.

At that moment, the lights went out, and all the power in the cabin fizzed off.

"And that, I'm afraid, was the power," he added. Since it was daytime, it wasn't dark. But the leaden gray light outside didn't make things very bright. And the white falling snow was like a curtain closing in around us. The cabin suddenly seemed gray, and colder.

Karen gave a little shriek. "Are we trapped?

Is the monster in the snow going to come and take us away?"

"Like in the movie?" David Michael's voice rose.

"We are not trapped," said his mother firmly. "In fact, we're about to go into town for some more food and supplies, and I think you younger kids should come with us." In the dim light, I could see her eyes meet Watson's, and see Watson nod.

"We'll take the station wagon," Watson said. "It has four-wheel drive."

"That means it can drive anywhere, even through the worst snow," Kristy told her stepsister.

Karen said, with relish, "If we get lost in the snow, we can just live in the station wagon until they find us. Or until spring."

"We're not going to get lost, Karen," said Watson. "And the roads are kept clear even in the worst weather. But bundle up warmly now."

Claudia said, "We'll help you guys get ready." She and I followed Karen to her bunk. Abby caught on and went with David Michael and Andrew, leaving Kristy with her family to go over any details, such as what to do if the blizzard really did bury the cabin.

When we returned, Watson had left to pull

the station wagon up to the door. We went out onto the porch with Kristy and Sam and Charlie, and the kids climbed into the station wagon.

Kristy's mom turned and said, "Remember, if it gets too bad, you can go to the lodge. But don't try to go if you can't see your way or find the trail. The phone lines will be back up soon. So will the power."

"Don't worry, Mom," said Sam. "I'm here." He flexed his arm like one of those nerd body builders in the backs of magazines.

I rolled my eyes.

Just then a voice said, "Hey! You're not leaving, are you?"

We looked up. "It's that guy we saw at the lodge yesterday, Woodie Keenan," said Abby softly. "He has a cabin nearby."

Woodie Keenan was bundled up so you could barely see him. I suddenly shivered, realizing how cold I felt.

"Just going into town for a few things," said Mrs. Brewer. "Do you need anything?"

"Firewood," said Woodie. "I'm running low, and so is the lodge."

"We're running low ourselves. We'll be glad to pick some up for you too," Mrs. Brewer assured him. "And we'll be back before very long."

"Thanks," said Woodie. "See you later."

We watched as Woodie disappeared down the trail, then waved good-bye as the station wagon disappeared into the swirling snow.

It seemed darker. And colder. I realized that the day was fading away as the blizzard grew stronger.

"We're almost out of wood," said Charlie. "I think we should bundle up so we don't use as much."

We huddled around the fire for awhile. We couldn't make hot chocolate or coffee because there was no electricity. And it wasn't easy to see in the gray gloom that was enveloping the cabin.

Suddenly Claudia lifted her head. "What was that?"

"What? I didn't hear anything," I said.

"I heard something. Outside."

"The wind," said Kristy impatiently.

Sam said, "There's a little more wood outside under the porch by the back stairs. We should bring it inside and put it near the fire to stay dry."

"Good idea," I said. I was going crazy just sitting there. I jumped up. "I'll go get some."

"I'll go with you," said Sam.

What could I say? More important, what was Sam going to say?

We went out onto the back porch. I put my hand out and touched Sam's arm. I took a deep breath. "Sam. Listen. I like you as a friend. I really do. But Robert and I are serious."

Sam looked surprised. "I know," he said.

"I know you and your girlfriend broke up, and I, well, I can't really see us getting back together," I continued.

"Us? Us who?" asked Sam, looking even more surprised.

I felt like a big dope. Had I misinterpreted Sam's actions?

"Us, as in you and me . . ." My voice trailed off.

Sam stared at me. Then to my surprise he blushed.

"Stacey!" he said. His voice was reproachful. "I still like you. A lot. But I think of you as a friend, someone who is fun to goof with. Someone I can be myself with. Sort of a, uh," he ducked his head, "best girl friend, but not girlfriend, you know?"

"Oh," I said stupidly. I was relieved. And humiliated. How conceited of me.

Then Sam made me feel better. "But I do like to flirt with you," he said. "It keeps me in practice for my next girlfriend."

"Oh, you," I said, swatting him on the arm.

Then I linked my arm through his and we trudged down the back steps.

The snow seemed to be slacking off for a moment. But the sky was darker than ever. I was amazed at how quickly the drifts around the door had piled up.

Sam and I waded off the steps toward the wood under the porch.

Then I stopped. I opened my mouth but no sound came out. I pointed.

Sam looked in the direction I was pointing.

The swirling, shifting snow was already covering it, but there was no mistaking what it was.

Blood in the snow.

I shrieked.

When I shrieked, Sam jumped and made a strangled sound.

It was enough to bring everybody running out onto the porch.

"What's wrong?" asked Kristy.

We both pointed. "Blood!" I managed to say.

Charlie walked along the edge of the porch and so did Claud. They bent over the railing of the porch and peered down at the gruesome spot in the snow.

Charlie shook his head. "Looks like some

poor bird bought it," he said. "A fox probably got it, although they are usually pretty shy and don't come out until later in the day or evening."

"A f-fox?" I asked, through stiff lips.

"Yup. You can see a couple of footprints under the edge of the porch here. And some feathers. Take a look."

"Thanks," I said, "but I'll take your word for it."

Everybody else hustled back inside. I helped Sam fill his arms with logs. Then I walked around the porch and stared out at the woods. I could barely see the nearby trees in the blinding whiteness. The snow had started coming down again, heavier than ever. The wind and snow were already erasing our footprints by the back steps.

And the blood in the snow.

I reached the front of the house, and stopped. The skis that we'd carefully set back against the wall of the porch the day before were still there. Everything looked as it should.

Except for the ski poles that stood upright in the snow on either side of the front steps.

Kristy's ski poles. The ones with the monograms on them that we'd teased her about.

There they stood. They hadn't been there when Watson and Elizabeth had left. We would have seen them.

I stared, and I felt very cold. Colder than the snow that swirled around me.

The ski poles had been snapped neatly in half.

And there were no footprints leading to them, or away.

I turned to go inside, trying to act calm, as if it were no big deal. We *had* heard somebody outside the house. It hadn't just been the sound of a fox killing a small animal.

Something moved in the trees.

I made a mad dash for the door, flung myself inside, and slammed the door behind me.

Everyone looked up.

"Stacey?" said Claudia.

"What is it?" asked Abby.

I motioned for my friends to follow me into the girls' bedroom.

"Lock the doors," I panted. "Close the windows. Your ski poles . . . somebody . . . outside . . ."

I took a deep breath. "Your ski poles are outside in the snow, Kristy," I said. "Someone has been here and broken them. I thought

Mary Anne said something about Karl Tate before the lines went dead. But it's not him. It's her. Kris Renn. I just saw Kris Renn sneaking around in the trees. And I'm pretty sure she has a gun."

CHAPTER 18

Shannon

Sunday

The phones at Shadow Lake were out. We didn't know whether Stacey had heard everything Mary Anne had said to her. What could we do? We weren't even sure we were right, anyway. Maybe it was the petnapper, and maybe not.

I just hoped everyone would stay together, up there in the woods.

Mal's mother arrived in one of the Pike-mobiles (the Pikes own *two* station wagons) to take Mal and Jessi back to the Pikes' to finish up their weekend baby-sitting assignment. The mystery seemed to have driven away Mal's grudge against insulation. She only groaned slightly when Mrs. Pike started talking about how much warmer the house was already.

Then she looked sideways at Jessi and they both started to giggle.

That left me with Logan and Mary Anne, who were not, I could tell, getting along. They kept looking at each other, then looking away, starting sentences and interrupting each other. It was *very* uncomfortable.

"Let's take Astrid for a walk," I said, just to get out of the house. Astrid is our Bernese mountain dog.

"It's snowing again," said Mary Anne, staring at her shoe.

"Astrid won't mind the snow," Logan said, looking at a point over the top of Mary Anne's head.

"She *loves* it," I said. "It makes her act like a puppy, and we can walk over to the Tates' house. It isn't far from here."

Mary Anne and Logan came along without

further argument — with me or with each other. Astrid was delighted, and although she is very well behaved on a leash, she kept making wuffling noises of delight, burying her nose in the snow and snorting.

The Tates' house, surveillance wise, was kind of a disappointment from the outside. It was a mansion (we are definitely the mansion neighborhood) and it was set back from the road. A "FOR SALE" sign was stuck in the front yard, crooked and half hidden by the snow. The paint on the gates at the foot of the driveway was chipped and peeling. The hedges on either side of the gate were overgrown. The curtains at the windows were drawn.

The house sat on a corner lot. We circled around to the other street. From the side, we could see the garage door standing open, and the garage was empty. No red Mercedes, no anything else.

"Maybe neither of them is home," I said.

"Looks that way," said Logan.

The only thing moving in the whole landscape was a cat, walking in that disgusted-cat way through the wet snow toward the back of the house.

Astrid hadn't been out all day. That's my excuse for her. One minute she was being a Good Dog. The next minute she'd jerked the leash from my hand, crashed through a thin place in the hedge, and was tearing across the backyard.

The cat took one look at her and abandoned its injured dignity to go into cat hyperspeed. It disappeared through the back door of the house. I realized a pet door must be there.

Astrid realized it, too.

"Astrid!" I shouted. She didn't even look back. She just squeezed herself through the pet door and into the house.

"We shouldn't be doing this," said Mary Anne nervously.

"No one's around," I said. "The neighbors can't see us. And it's not like we're breaking in."

"This door is open!" said Logan in surprise. "Look."

"Someone could be waiting on the other side," Mary Anne said.

"I hope Astrid is." I could envision the damage Astrid was doing, racing around someone's house, chasing a cat. I'd already tried calling her through the pet door, but to no avail. And none of us was quite small enough to fit through it. It must have been a tight squeeze for Astrid.

The door opened directly into a kitchen, big

and shiny and spotless, and unused looking. We went from there into a hall.

"Astrid," I called softly, in case someone *was* home and had managed somehow not to hear the commotion of a dog chasing a cat into their house.

One door opened into an office, or what was left of an office. Dusty cherrywood file cabinets lined one wall. A huge, worn leather chair was pushed tightly against a massive cherrywood desk. Glass front bookshelves were filled with books. On one wall was a surveyor's map of Stoneybrook, with various colored push pins stuck into it.

Everything was dusty, and half-opened boxes filled with files were stacked around the room in no particular order. A bunch of framed pictures were propped against one wall. The wallpaper showed lighter patches, where the pictures had hung. The skeleton of a dead ficus tree stood at rigid attention in one corner.

"Karl Tate's office?" said Logan, walking to the desk. He picked a card from a little brass card holder. "Yeah. Look. Karl Tate, real estate. It rhymes."

"Thank you, Logan. Now, can we get out of here?" Mary Anne walked into the room behind Logan.

"Aren't we supposed to be investigating?" asked Logan.

"Not by breaking into somebody else's house."

"The door was open," said Logan. "So technically we're not even breaking in."

"Now you're a lawyer?" asked Mary Anne crossly, putting her hands on her hips, her voice rising. "Quick. Let me make a *note*!"

I stepped inside. "Guys! Shhh!"

Just then Astrid came careening out of nowhere. The cat streaked by, shot under the desk, banked off one of the walls, and streaked out again.

"Grab her!" I cried.

Logan and Mary Anne lunged for Astrid, and I slammed the door shut quickly so she couldn't take off again.

"Ha! Gotcha," I said.

I took Astrid's leash and she sat down demurely, her expression saying, "Me? Chase a cat? Never!"

"You're in trouble, you big furball," I told her. She wagged her tail and I laughed. "Oh, well. I guess all's well that end's well." I glanced up at Mary Anne and Logan (who looked like cats faced off against one another). "Let's get out of here."

I turned to open the door.

Shannon

Only it wouldn't open.

I twisted the knob. I gave it a jerk. I checked to make sure I hadn't somehow locked it. It held fast.

Logan, who had rushed to me, said, "Let me try."

But he didn't have any better luck.

Mary Anne tried. I tried again. We all tried together.

The door didn't budge.

"The windows," said Mary Anne. We made a mad dash for the big windows. But security locks were built into the latches, the kind that have to be opened with a key. Of course there was no key around anywhere, not on the shelves, not in the desk.

"The phone," I said. "We can use the phone to call someone to come let us out." I grabbed the receiver.

But the phone had been disconnected. I guess since Karl Tate wasn't in business anymore, he didn't need it.

Mary Anne went back to the door and tried again to open it. But it was no use.

We were trapped.

CHAPTER 19

Claudia

Sunday

I am never waching another scarry movie as long as I live. Or even readding a scarry book (except nancy Drew). Becaus its not just madeup any moor. Ive been traped in a house with a moneiac ortside...

"The phone is still dead," I said, putting down the receiver. "Way, way dead."

"Could you put it some other way, Claud? Please?" asked Stacey, glancing nervously at the broken ski poles that were leaning in the corner. (Kristy had insisted we bring them in and use gloves to touch them "in case there were fingerprints.")

The blizzard had reached full roar — literally — outside. The wind was howling, driving the snow almost parallel to the ground, at blinding speed.

And it was getting later and darker by the minute.

"Are the doors and windows all locked?" I asked. "Tell me they are."

"If they're not, they will be," said Kristy. "Let's go."

"We can't split up!" I practically shrieked. "That's what happens in horror movies, so the people can be picked off one by one."

Everyone looked at me. Then Abby said, "We can split up into *teams* and each take one side of the house."

We walked around the house. Some of the windows had locks. Some didn't. Abby and Kristy went outside and closed the shutters on the ones that didn't. Which of course made it even darker inside.

And we were too late anyway.

We'd just settled in by the fire when Stacey came back from the bathroom with a funny expression on her face. "Kristy," she said. "Could you come here a minute?"

A moment later, I heard Kristy exclaim, "Oh, no! Stacey . . ."

Stacey's insulin was missing. It had been taken right out of the little case in the inside pocket of her suitcase.

"Ohmigosh, Stacey!" I exclaimed.

"Don't worry," she said quickly. "I always carry a spare case in my backpack. But someone had to come in and take it out. I've looked everywhere."

I sat down heavily on the bed.

And saw the feathers.

I leaped up with a little gasp.

I don't know what I thought. Maybe that someone had killed a small animal on my bed.

It wasn't that. But it was just as creepy.

My pillow had been slit open, end to end. Its insides were spilling out across my bed. Claudia's red nail polish had been emptied on top. It was still sticky.

I put my hand over my mouth. I felt sick with fear. Someone had been here, in this room, maybe even while we were sitting in the next room by the fire.

The stalker had found us at Shadow Lake. And he was getting closer.

Dangerously close.

Okay. It was me. I insisted that we search the house to make sure the "maniac" wasn't inside. We checked out every possible inch. Subtly. So that Sam and Charlie kept playing checkers without noticing.

Kristy said, "That's it. No one under the sink or behind the garbage can. Unless there's a secret door — "

The knock made us jump.

It was Woodie, covered to his eyebrows with snow.

"How did you get here?" demanded Kristy suspiciously.

Woodie pointed to his showshoes. "I found a little extra wood in my basement, so I thought I'd bring some over."

Kristy looked ashamed.

Charlie said, "Thanks. It doesn't look as though Watson and Mom are going to make it back from town anytime soon. Maybe not before tomorrow."

"You might want to head up to the lodge," said Woodie. "Before it gets worse."

The words sounded innocent enough, but they made me shudder inwardly. How much worse could it be?

"Not yet," said Charlie, glancing from Sam to Kristy and then back at Woodie. "We want to stay here in case they do try to make it back. You want to come in and warm up?"

"Thanks, but I need to head back to my own cabin," said Woodie. "I left the fire burning. Wouldn't want the whole place to burn down." He shook his head. "That's a little too warm for me."

He turned to leave. We stepped back inside. But as I was closing the door, something made me stop. I frowned. From the back, Woodie looked familiar. Very, very familiar. In a chilling kind of way.

Then I remembered Stacey's words: "Mary Anne said something about Karl Tate before the lines went dead."

Karl Tate. The petnapper.

From the back, Woodie Keenan looked just like a young Karl Tate.

I slammed the door and turned around. "Hey, guys!" I shouted.

Claudia

"Open the door!" screamed Kristy.

"No! Keep it closed!" shouted Sam. "It'll only make the fire worse!"

That's when I realized the cabin was filled with smoke.

CHAPTER 20

LOGAN

SUNDAY

EVERY PICTURE TELLS A STORY. PUT
YOURSELF IN THE PICTURE. A PICTURE
IS WORTH A THOUSAND WORDS. PICTURE
THIS. TAKE A LOOK AT THE BIG PICTURE.
NOW I GET THE PICTURE. . . .

We were locked in the old office of Karl Tate's house, which would make anybody nervous. But Mary Anne was acting worse than nervous. She was, for her, acting almost mean. No matter what I said, or what I did, she took a shot at me.

I admit, I took some shots at her, too.

Meanwhile, Shannon had tactfully moved away from us — at least, as far away as she could without leaving the room. She squatted to examine the pictures propped against the wall.

"Hey," she said. "Look. The Tate family." She held up a framed photograph of a man, a woman, and a little boy, all dressed up and smiling. "Look at her hair. It must be an old photograph."

We barely glanced at it. We were busy glaring at each other.

Shannon put the photograph down and stood up. "That's it," she said. "I've had it. Either have your fight and clear the air, or at least say what's on your mind."

"Nothing's on my mind," I said loftily.

"You can say that again," snapped Mary Anne.

"Stop it!" said Shannon.

I looked at Mary Anne. Her voice was angry,

but her eyes were filling with tears. Hurt tears.

What was going on? I couldn't take it any longer.

I broke down and told Shannon about the notes.

Mary Anne laughed!

That made me see red. I glared at her and she took a quick step back. "Oh, Logan," she said. "I'm not laughing about the notes. I didn't send them to you. I'm laughing because someone's been sending *me* notes, too. And they looked like they were in *your* handwriting!"

Well, it didn't take long after that to sort things out, and realize that she and I had both been the victims of some kind of nasty prank. Mary Anne thought it was Cokie's doing. I wasn't so sure.

But it didn't matter anyway. What mattered was that we weren't having a stupid fight over a stupid misunderstanding. Completely forgetting about Shannon, I leaned over and kissed Mary Anne.

Shannon said, "This is great and all, but in case you two have forgotten, we *are* still locked in the Tates' house."

I straightened up quickly and Mary Anne blushed a deep crimson.

"Well, since we're here," I said, "we might as well keep investigating."

We went over the room (after checking the door one more time), looking in drawers and on shelves. But nothing very interesting turned up until I started going through the wastepaper basket. I grabbed a handful of papers out of it and spread them on the desk. Mary Anne snatched one up. "Shadow Lake," she said. "This is the area code and phone number for Kristy's cabin at Shadow Lake. The one I just called!"

"That's not all," I said. I held up another piece of paper, a photocopy of an article from the *Stoneybrook News*.

It was the picture of the BSC after they'd helped to capture Karl Tate. A big, black X had been drawn viciously across it, so hard that the paper had torn.

"It *is* him," said Mary Anne in a shaky voice. "Oh, Logan."

"Shhh," said Shannon. "Do you hear that?"

We heard.

A car was pulling into the driveway.

CHAPTER 21

Abby

Sunday

Did I ask for this?
When I joined the BSC,
I wanted a job, some
friends. By friends, I
did not mean acquaint-
ances in low places. You
know, like maniacs.
And convicted felons...

Abby

It wasn't a fire drill. It was real. At least, the smoke was. The fire, fortunately, stayed in the fireplace. The smoke didn't. It poured out of the chimney in big, black, oily clouds. I had to dash out onto the porch to breathe, and take a hit on my inhaler. Fortunately, it didn't trigger a full scale asthma attack, just my standard allergic reaction to Life. Woodie had heard the commotion and come running back up the trail to help.

I was sneezing and wheezing (a little) when Stacey and Claudia and Kristy came reeling outside, throwing the door open. Smoke billowed out behind them and was immediately blown away by the gale.

Kristy had to raise her voice (which tells you just how loudly the wind was blowing) to be heard.

"Someone blocked the chimney," she said. "We've put out the fire, but we're not going to be able to start a new one. With no electricity, that means no heat."

"The lodge?" I suggested.

"The lodge," Kristy agreed. "We'll pack up just what we need for the night and go as soon as there's a break in the storm."

Claudia said, in an urgent undertone, "Remember what Mary Anne said to you, Stacey? Karl Tate?"

Stacey nodded.

"Well, right before the smoke started, I thought I saw him."

Stacey and Kristy looked startled. Then Kristy said, "He's in jail, Claudia. Whoever's after us, it's not him."

"I didn't say I saw him. I said I *thought* I saw him. Woodie Keenan looks just like him from behind. And you know, in detective stories, they say that you can't disguise the way someone looks from behind. The way they stand and walk always gives them away."

Kristy said, "But I don't think Woodie is wearing a disguise. How could Karl Tate make himself look that young?"

Charlie said, "Kristy. You guys! Let's get going."

"I know what I saw," Claudia said stubbornly.

"What you thought you saw," said Kristy. She paused. "We need to tell Charlie and Sam what's going on. But let's concentrate on getting out of here first. We'll tell them at the lodge." She ran into the house where Charlie and Sam and Woodie were waiting.

I waited until the place had aired out some,

then went inside and packed my knapsack. Fortunately, there was a break in the storm, enough to see the trail along the lake and the bright blue *Shadow Lake* trail markers.

"Stay together," Charlie said sternly. He handed around the flashlights "just in case," while Kristy packed the emergency flares in her backpack. She also put matches in watertight bags and zipped those into the pocket of her ski parka.

Charlie went on, "If you lose sight of the person ahead of you, yell immediately. And *loudly*. And don't go off the trail. Shadow Lake is frozen, but it is dangerous. There's lots of thin ice above the underground springs that feed it."

He didn't have to warn us twice. I personally planned on staying right on top of whoever was in front of me. Abby of the Yukon I am not.

I saw Sam pat Stacey reassuringly on the shoulder. Stacey didn't jump or act startled. Hmmm. Must have worked that one out, I thought.

It was slow, hard going. The snow was over the tops of my snow boots. I had laced them over my pants legs and put on my ski pants for extra warmth, but I could feel the snow seeping in and melting, and making my clothes cold and wet. We had to lift our feet high for each step. I tried to step into Claudia's footprints, since she was walking ahead of me. Poor Charlie, I thought. Being the trailbreaker couldn't be any fun.

Amazing that the snow had filled up Woodie Keenan's snowshoe tracks so fast. Charlie could have used those.

Something crashed through the woods behind me. Claudia looked over her shoulder. Her eyes widened. "Abby! Look out! It's him! It's *Karl Tate!*"

And from out of the swirling whiteness of the blizzard, a dark form hurtled toward us from behind. He shouted something I couldn't understand.

I stooped, grabbed a chunk of ice, and threw it at him. It clocked him right in the head. He reeled back and fell. His face looked truly deranged.

That won't stop him long, I thought frantically. I wasn't going to be able to hold him off with snowballs. I needed a rock. A big rock. Or maybe a big stick. I looked around desperately.

"*Run!*" screamed Claudia.

And then someone else came running through the woods from one side.

"Freeze!" a voice ordered. *"Don't move!"*

Kris Renn skidded to a stop in a spray of snow, and half-crouched, her arms up and her hands gripping a gun.

I let go of the branch I had grabbed (unfortunately, it was still attached to the tree) and held up my hands.

Karl Tate didn't move. Slowly, Renn took one hand off the gun and reached in her pocket. She pulled out a badge. "Detective Kris Renn," she said to me. "Special Unit. Put your hands down. It's him I'm interested in."

"It *was* you I saw in the woods with a gun," Stacey said.

"I've been on his trail for some time," Detective Renn explained. "He's violated the terms of his parole by leaving Connecticut, among other things." She bent over, put handcuffs on him, and sat him upright. She looked at the red mark on his head. "Hmm," she said, glancing at me. "Good aim."

"I'm the assistant coach of a softball team," I said inanely.

Kristy snorted. And then we all started laughing. It was such a relief. It had been Karl Tate after all. Karl Tate had been stalking the

BSC, paying back the members who'd helped catch him by terrorizing them.

Funny. He didn't look like a terrorist, sagging against Detective Renn. He looked old and tired.

"I hope I didn't hurt him," I said.

As if in answer, he groaned. His eyelids fluttered.

"Do you need help?" Stacey asked Renn.

The detective said, "I can handle it. My cabin's just down this trail. I'll take him there until this storm blows over. I can radio the situation in."

"Cool," said Claudia.

"Would someone mind telling me what's going on?" asked Charlie.

"Well," said Kristy.

Woodie asked, "Is this a joke?"

"Tell us at the lodge," said Charlie.

Detective Renn hauled Mr. Tate to his feet. He reeled like a drunken man on a subway train.

"Be careful," she told us.

"We will," I said. I flexed my arm. "How about that pitch?" I boasted.

Claudia said, "You are such a show-off." But she was grinning. We were all relieved that Karl Tate had been caught. Now we could continue our weekend without fear.

"I'm planning on entering the Olympic Ice Hurling Event," I said.

"Oh, brother," said Kristy, and we set off down the trail for the lodge.

CHAPTER 22

Mary Anne

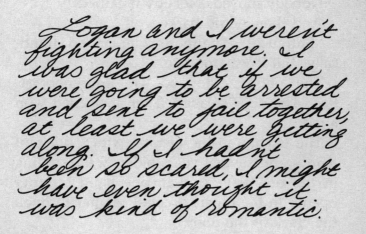

Logan and I weren't fighting anymore. I was glad that if we were going to be arrested and sent to jail together, at least we were getting along. If I hadn't been so scared, I might have even thought it was kind of romantic.

MaryAnne

"Hide!" hissed Shannon.

We all dove for hiding places. I jumped behind the door. Logan crouched down behind a chair, and Shannon and Astrid crawled under the desk.

The kitchen door opened.

Had Mr. Tate come back? What would he do to us if he caught us?

Footsteps clicked down the hall.

Nobody moved. Nobody breathed.

And then Astrid barked.

"Shhhush!" Shannon commanded frantically. But it was too late.

The footsteps stopped. The doorknob rattled. The door creaked. Then it opened with a jerk.

The woman in the picture, with a different hairdo and several years older, was standing in the doorway, mail in one hand, a letter opener in the other. (I could see her through the crack of the door.)

"Who's there?" she said sharply.

Slowly, Shannon came out from under the desk, holding Astrid's leash. Logan crawled out from behind the chair. I peered around the door.

Mrs. Tate gasped and jumped back. The letter opener and the mail fell from her hands. Logan swooped down and grabbed the letter opener, but Mrs. Tate didn't seem to notice. Her attention was fastened on me.

"It's you," she said. "You're one of the girls! From that club."

I nodded. My heart was pounding so hard I could hear it in my ears.

Mrs. Tate seemed dazed. She walked across the room and sat in the chair. She put her head in her hands.

"Mrs. Tate?" I said. "We're — we're sorry. We didn't mean to . . ."

With a sound like a moan, Mrs. Tate looked up. Her eyes filled with tears and I felt tears well up in my own eyes.

But what she said stopped my tears. "You have to stop him," she said hoarsely. "You have to stop him!"

"Mr. Tate?" I asked.

"No! No, not Karl. Woodrow. My son."

I remembered the boy in the picture. He must be grown by now, I realized.

Shannon started edging toward the door. Logan put the letter opener down on the desk and caught my hand. We began to follow Shannon and Astrid.

"We're sorry about coming into your house,"

Shannon said. "I mean, uninvited. It was an accident. My dog, Astrid? She chased your cat in through the pet door."

"Miss Kitty," murmured Mrs. Tate. "That's our cat's name."

"Um, yeah. Anyway, we, uh — The back door was open and we came in, just to catch Astrid, but we got locked in the study."

"I have to have that lock fixed," Mrs. Tate said. "But since Karl . . . went away . . ."

She focused on me again. "Stop him," she said. "Stop Woodrow. I should've. I should have called the police. But I couldn't. I just couldn't." She buried her face in her hands again.

"I'm sorry," I said again, awkwardly.

Mrs. Tate didn't seem to hear. Logan tugged at my hand.

We turned and walked as quickly as we could out of the house.

It had gotten so late.

"We have to call Kristy," I said urgently. "We have to warn her."

"We have to call the police," said Shannon.

We ran for the nearest pay phone. Someone paged Sergeant Johnson. When he came to the phone at last, we told him what we'd found out.

As calmly as ever, the sergeant said, "Very

good. Don't worry. I'll take care of everything."

I hung up, feeling drained.

"Call Kristy," Shannon urged me.

We pooled all our change and I called the Shadow Lake number.

But still there was no answer.

I hung up slowly.

We'd done all we could do. But what if it wasn't enough? What if Sergeant Johnson didn't warn Kristy and the others in time?

What was Woodrow Tate planning to do?

CHAPTER 23

Kristy

This is a pun for Abby: the BSC ^(Sunday) knows how to solve mysteries with a flare.

Get it, Abby? Flare.

It was growing dark sooo fast. I trudged along behind Charlie, glad the mystery was solved, glad the terror was over, and wishing more than anything for a warm, dry, quiet place. I was thinking hot chocolate. I was thinking nachos. These were thoughts of which I was sure the others would approve, especially Claud.

I was not thinking danger.

We flicked on our flashlights. They barely pricked the growing darkness and the swirling snow. "I'm going to light a flare or two," I said.

We stopped. Sam said, "Why don't a couple of us go on ahead?"

"Sounds like a good idea," said Woodie.

Abby said, "And warn the people at the lodge that a very large, very cold, very hungry party is coming in from the wilderness. I volunteer!"

Since the lodge was just around the bend ahead, I wasn't worried about them getting lost or separated from us. I lit a flare and handed it to Abby. "Go for it," I said to Abby and Sam.

As they plunged out of sight, I lit the other two flares and gave one of them to Charlie.

"We're almost there," I said encouragingly. "You go first and I'll bring up the rear."

Kristy

We fell into line: Charlie, Stacey, Woodie, Claudia, and me. The flares helped, but they made weird shadows in the ghostly swirl of the snow.

To one side I could see the drop down to the lake. To the other, the trees marched up the hillside, twisting and moaning in the wind.

I thought of the dumb horror movie Karen and David Michael had been watching.

Stacey suddenly seemed to slip. Woodie leaped forward, in the same instant, and grabbed her wrist. But he didn't pull her away from the lake to safety. He pulled her toward him, toward the lake, backing into the shelter of a tree.

Claudia stopped. We all stopped.

What was going on?

Then Stacey screamed, "What are you doing? Let me go!"

And Woodie began to laugh.

"Stay back," he shouted. "Stand back or she goes in!"

We stopped in a ragged half-circle around him.

"Woodie?" said Charlie. "What — ?"

"Shut up!" screamed Woodie. His eyes rolled wildly. "It's your fault. You made me do it. You're the ones who caused all the trouble!"

"What are you talking about?" I said.

"My father. Karl Tate — "

"Karl Tate!" Claudia said with a gasp.

"Remember him?" Woodie's lip lifted in a sneer. "Or have you already forgotten how you ruined him? Humiliated him. Sent him to prison!"

"But we didn't," I said. "We just — "

"Don't try to get out of it. Oh, you were big heroes, weren't you? Had your picture in the newspapers! Well, so did my father. Everyone pointed and stared and whispered. Suddenly we had nothing. Nothing! Do you know what that's like?"

Something caught my eye. A flare. It was Sam and Abby hurrying back toward us. Had they heard Stacey scream?

The flare disappeared. Then I saw them again, ghostly shapes crouched low, sneaking up behind Woodie, his arm now around Stacey's throat.

"We're sorry," I said, stalling for time.

"Not as sorry as you're going to be," he snarled.

Sam straightened up. He motioned at me. Then Abby made a throwing motion.

Woodie stepped back.

"No!" I shouted and threw my flare at him. Instinctively he raised his hands and ducked.

Stacey drove her elbow into Woodie's stomach and jumped away.

Woodie staggered back and slipped. For a moment, his arms flailed the air wildly. Sam grabbed for him, but it was too late.

With a wild, mad scream that I will never forget, Woodie Tate fell down the bank and through the ice into the freezing waters of Shadow Lake.

"It's over," I said. "This time, it's really over."

We were sitting in the lodge by the fire, surrounded by hot chocolate, nachos, and every combination of junk food we could lay our hands on. We were warm and dry and fed and safe. And Watson and Mom and Karen and Andrew and David Michael, escorted by the Shadow Lake police, were on their way back to the lodge to join us.

We had been trying to reach Woodie, who was thrashing in the lake, when Kris Renn came running up the trail behind us. At the same time, the sound of snowmobiles was followed by the appearance, from the direction of the lodge, of the Shadow Lake police.

Karl Tate had regained consciousness and told Detective Renn his story — how his son, unable to endure the shame and the poverty his father's actions had caused, had become obsessed with the BSC, blaming them for his family's troubles. By the time Mr. Tate was released from jail, Woodie was beyond control and had already embarked on his mad campaign of terror.

Then he'd disappeared, and Mr. Tate had found out where he'd gone. He didn't know what Woodie planned to do to the BSC members, but he feared the worst.

The Shadow Lake police, alerted by Sergeant Johnson, were more than willing to haul Woodie from the lake and take him off to the local jail. I assumed he was warm and dry now, too. And behind bars.

Our creepiest case ever was solved.

EPILOGUE

Watson and my mom were not too thrilled when they heard the story. I almost got in trouble for not telling them. But how could I have? I hadn't wanted to worry Watson. Or my mother, for that matter.

And what good would it have done?

Watson wanted to return to Stoneybrook immediately, like that night. But the blizzard ruled, and we ended up staying at the lodge. That was cool. It was sort of like a big party. Everyone there hung out and talked and, of course, we told everyone about our adventures. We went to bed early, though. Capturing criminals and solving mysteries is tiring.

On Monday morning we were greeted by excellent news from home: Nannie called to say that it was a snow day, so we weren't even going to miss school. (Claudia didn't think it was so excellent. She pointed out that if we had missed a day of school, we wouldn't have to make it up, but we often had to make up snow days at the end of the year.)

After a big breakfast, we checked on the cabin. Watson made arrangements with Mitch for some repairs and improvements (including locks on the windows). Then we set out for home.

Once we were off the back roads, the main roads were amazingly clear. We arrived home before lunch.

Did we hold the regular meeting of the BSC that afternoon? We did. Neither rain nor snow nor sleet nor criminals can stop the BSC. Logan and Shannon came, too, to hear our adventures, mostly.

"No charges are going to be filed against Noah Seger, Sergeant Johnson told me," Mary Anne reported as we all groaned and handed over our weekly dues to Stacey. "I called the police station and he said Noah is going to go to family counseling with his father. His friend is going for counseling, too."

"And Woodrow Tate has made a full confession," said Stacey. She tucked the envelope with our dues away and said, "Isn't that what Detective Renn said, Kristy?"

I nodded. Naturally I'd called the detective the moment we'd arrived home. "I can't believe we thought it was her, even for a second."

"I can," said Stacey. "She was acting oddly. And she did have a gun."

"What about the guy with the eyepatch?" Abby reminded us.

We laughed about that. We'd found out at the lodge the night before that he had been coming there for years — and complaining for years. This year, at least one of his complaints had been legitimate. He'd lost his ski bag (which later turned up in the lost and found).

"I was right," said Claudia. "I did see Karl Tate. His son walks just like him." She stuck her nose in the air. "It's the artist's superior eye for detail."

Jessi whacked her with a pillow and Claudia laughed.

"What I want to know," said Logan, changing the subject, "is who's been writing those notes to Mary Anne and me? It wasn't Woodrow Tate, that much we know."

Shannon said, "You should put them in the mystery notebook. Looks like we still have a mystery for the BSC."

"Speaking of notebooks, Mal, you did an awesome job," Jessi said.

We all agreed, and Mal ducked her head, looking pleased.

Then the phone rang, and it was business as usual.

When we'd taken care of the call, Claudia sighed happily and bit into a Dove chocolate bar. "It was an awesome vacation," she said.

"Yeah," said Abby, trying hard to keep a straight face. "Interesting. Diverting. Entertaining. Awesome. But listen, if we're going to keep up this mystery business, can I ask a favor? No pictures in the paper. Please!"

About the Author

ANN MATTHEWS MARTIN was born on August 12,
1955. She grew up in Princeton, NJ, with her parents and her younger sister, Jane.

In addition to the Baby-sitters Club books, Ann
has written many other books for children. Her
favorite is *Ten Kids, No Pets* because she loves big
families and she loves animals. Her favorite Baby-
sitters Club book is *Kristy's Big Day.*

Ann M. Martin now lives in New York with
her cats, Gussie and Woody. Her hobbies are reading, sewing, and needlework — especially making
clothes for children.

THE BABY-SITTERS CLUB®

by Ann M. Martin

Available wherever you buy books...or use this order form.

Scholastic Inc., P.O. Box 7502, 2931 E. McCarty Street, Jefferson City, MO 65102

Please send me the books I have checked above. I am enclosing $ _____
(please add $2.00 to cover shipping and handling). Send check or money order—no
cash or C.O.D.s please.

Name _____ Birthdate _____

Address _____

City _____ State/Zip _____

Please allow four to six weeks for delivery. Offer good in the U.S. only. Sorry, mail orders are not
available to residents of Canada. Prices subject to change.

THE BABY-SITTERS CLUB®

Meet the best friends you'll ever have!

by Ann M. Martin

ALL NEW!

Have you heard? The BSC has a new look—and more great stuff than ever before. An all-new scrapbook for each book's narrator! A letter from Ann M. Martin! Fill-in pages to personalize your copy! Order today!

☐ BBD22473-5	#1 **Kristy's Great Idea**	$3.50
☐ BBD22763-7	#2 **Claudia and the Phantom Phone Calls**	$3.50
☐ BBD25158-9	#3 **The Truth About Stacey**	$3.50
☐ BBD25159-7	#4 **Mary Anne Saves the Day**	$3.50
☐ BBD25160-0	#5 **Dawn and the Impossible Three**	$3.50

Available wherever you buy books, or use this order form.

■ SCHOLASTIC

BSCE395